W9-AZW-520

HERE

HERE

Stories by Elizabeth Inness-Brown

Louisiana State University Press
Baton Rouge and London
1994

Designer: Laura Roubique Gleason
Typeface: Bembo
Typesetter: G&S Typesetters, Inc.
Printer and binder: Thomson-Shore, Inc.

LIBRARY OF CONGRESS CATALOGING-IN-PUBLICATION DATA

Inness-Brown, Elizabeth, date.
    Here : stories / by Elizabeth Inness-Brown.
       p.   cm.
    ISBN 0-8071-1848-6
    I. Title
    PS3559.N47H47   1994
    813'.54—dc20   93-34588
                                                         CIP

The author offers grateful acknowledgment to the editors of the following
publications, in which stories in this book originally appeared in slightly different
form: *Boulevard* (Winter, 1986, Fall, 1988, and Fall, 1992), "Someone" (originally
entitled "Here"), "The Housesitter," and "The Chef's Bride"; *Cream City Review*
(Spring, 1994), "Territory"; *Glimmer Train* (Summer, 1992), "The Surgeon";
Mississippi Review (Spring–Summer, 1989), "Stephen"; *New Orleans Review*
(Summer, 1990), "Life in the Tropics"; *North American Review* (March, 1989),
"Traveler"; *St. Lawrence Magazine* (Summer, 1991), "Sleepwalker"; *Lo Spazio
Umano* (January, 1986), "Really Love Him"; *Sycamore Review* (Winter, 1990), "The
Sound." "Horse Dreams" originally appeared in *The New Yorker*.

Parts of this book were written with the support of a grant from the National
Endowment for the Arts.

This is dedicated to the one I love

"A slow sort of country!" said the Queen. "Now, *here,* you see, it takes all the running you can do, to keep in the same place. If you want to get somewhere else, you must run at least twice as fast as that!"

—Lewis Carroll, *Through the Looking Glass*

Contents

In its making, this book passed under many eyes and through many hands aside from my own. I owe thanks to Joe David Bellamy, mentor and friend; to fellow writers Barbara Floersch, Judy Goodrobb, and Dianne McKnight; and to my colleagues and students, from whom I have learned so much. I also thank Martha Hall, Catherine Landry, Barry Blose, and the other people at Louisiana State University Press for their excellent, professional, and untiring work. And finally, I offer thanks (small offering though it be) to my husband, Keith Monley, whose honesty, constancy, integrity, and love have meant and will always mean so much to me.

HERE

Territory

I was ten in 1954, the year my father got out of the air force and took my mother and me on our first vacation. All I remember of it is a trip to the zoo: the three of us walking hand in hand, looking at yellow polar bears and sleeping lions in cages; the three of us sitting on a slatted park bench, feeding bits of our hot-dog rolls to pigeons. There was snow on the ground, but the sun was out and the snow was melting.

When we got back, Daddy got a loan, and we moved out of the city and my grandparents' apartment and to a housing development in another town, and we bought a new car and our first television set. For a while we were happy.

Then one night we were back where we started. It was one of those nights when I made a tent of the covers and, shining my flashlight on a book stolen from my mother's night table, read with relish if only feathery understanding until the words began to parade across the pages like black ants. Then I got out of bed to hide the flashlight on the windowsill behind the curtain and the book between the mattress and box spring, where I would feel it all night, like the princess who felt the pea through her tower of mattresses.

But before I could climb back into bed, I heard the kitchen door open and the sound of voices. Within seconds the fight began. My father was home.

His new job was as a traveling salesman, and because of it he spent many nights on the road. It had taken me a while to understand that this didn't mean that he literally spent the night in his car pulled over on the shoulder somewhere, as I pictured him, but in hotels with neon lights. It didn't matter. It was really no different from the old days, when he sold door to door and we never knew for certain when he would be back. But until this night his coming home to this house had been a joyful occasion. This night Mama was mad because he hadn't called when he said he would, and he was mad that she didn't have anything for him to eat. But how it started and what they said had nothing to do with what it was about. Even at ten I knew that.

My bedroom door was open a crack so that Mama could hear me if I "needed" her, and through the crack, light from the hallway poured onto my blue carpet, pointing like an arrowhead into the hallway. I got up now and went to sit in the darkness beside the light, so I could see into the hall and hear them, but they could not see me. They had moved from the kitchen into the living room, yelling louder, screaming. Mama brought up my shoes: I only had two pair and she thought I should have more: shoes for school, shoes for church, shoes for play, rubber boots and winter boots, sandals . . . To hear her you'd think my shoe situation summed up everything my father had ever done wrong. My father said something about the car. "That damn car!" Mama screeched. "All you ever think about is that damn car!" "That damn car is my living now!" my father yelled back. "They gave me the biggest territory in the district, you know that!" "Goddamn your territory," Mama replied, and I heard the thump of something heavy hitting the floor, and knew Mama had thrown the thick glass ashtray they had been given as a wedding present—"the only indestructible thing in the house," Mama said. Then something flew down the hallway, bouncing off the wall and toward me until it was only a few inches outside my door. It was my father's watch. I wanted to reach my hand out and pick it up, but I thought they'd see me, and that thought filled me with fear the way cold water fills a pitcher.

The fight went on. I got back into bed and pulled my pillow over my head. It took a while for them to quiet down, and then a while more for me to go to sleep. I dreamed that I was with them in the new car, driving along a quiet country road. We had the top down, but my father was driving slow so that the summer air just seemed to envelop me, seemed to flow over my skin and through my hair like warm hands. They sat

2

close to each other in the front seat. Pleasant, wordless music played on the radio. In the back seat I stretched out my legs, put my hands behind my head so that my elbows stuck out, and leaned back, the way I'd seen men do in movies. I closed my eyes for hardly a second, but still when I opened them things had changed. The car was going faster, speeding up. The wind pulled at my clothes, and my hair whipped and tangled in front of my eyes. My parents seemed oblivious, their backs to me, motionless except for the movement of their own clothes and hair. The wind drowned out the music from the radio, but they seemed not to notice that either. My father's hands were relaxed on the steering wheel; he turned it gently, but still the car jerked this way and that. And suddenly in front of us a tree appeared. Its limbs hung heavy with fruit, but it wasn't a fruit tree; it was too tall, too big through the trunk, with smooth bark. I knew, the way you know things in dreams, that this tree had moved in front of us deliberately.

Somehow, when we struck it, we were thrown loose. The next thing I remember is standing there looking at the car, which was torn exactly down the middle like a car in a cartoon, ragged at the edges as if it had been made out of paper.

The next morning my father was gone again, but I thought he had just gone off to work. A week passed, and then two, and he didn't come back, and I knew he was really gone. My mother never said a word about it, or him; she just started to let me stay up later at night. After dinner I got into my nightgown and came and sat between her legs while she brushed my hair. Then I brushed hers. It sparked gold and seemed alive to me, the way it pulled itself out from under the bristles. We watched television together, me with my grubby, skinned knees pulled up under my nightgown and her with her long smooth-shaved legs folded beside her, her bare feet shiny and the skin tight over the bones. She had long, thin feet, and she kept her toenails filed and polished. She thought that her feet were her "best feature," but I thought she was beautiful all over, more like an elegant animal than an ordinary human woman, different from other mothers, with her long neck and lank body and the stark angles of her face.

3

She started to talk to me, as if with my father gone she needed someone else and had decided I was old enough to listen. She talked about going back to work. She wanted to be a secretary, she said, but she didn't think she could learn how to type well enough, fast enough. She didn't want to go back to waitressing. She hated everything about it. The frilly uniform looked funny on her, like a sweater on a dog. The food smell got in her, not just on her, she said; she said you couldn't wash it off, that smell of salad dressing and coffee grounds and the grease from charbroiled meat. She hated the shoes, the net they made her put over her hair, the customers: "Party of two, party of four, but it never was a party at all," she said. "Just men in suits trying to impress each other and their little women."

I thought about the restaurant where she'd worked. It was called the Golden Hog, and in the lobby of it was a giant gilded plaster-of-Paris pig. People made jokes about eating "high on the hog." It was a popular place. Until my father had come back, I'd walked there to wait for her after school, not wanting to go home to my grandmother sitting in the dingy apartment smoking cigarettes at the kitchen table. Besides, they had a television set in the bar, a hulking thing that sat in a corner, and I'd sit on a stool and watch Kukla, Fran, and Ollie, drinking some flat soda that the bartender gave me so that he could ignore me. It was always midafternoon and quiet. When she came out of the dining room, she'd slide me a tired look and sit there next to me in her ruffled apron and count her quarters and dimes and nickels, and change them for bills when there was enough. Sometimes, for the extra hours and tips, she'd work as a drink waitress at night, and because she didn't have to wear her uniform, she liked that better. But then she had to leave me with my grandparents, who didn't approve of her working and made me go to bed before dark. Still, who could she leave me with now, now that we were living here, in this development, far away from home?

I liked listening to her, I liked that she talked to me. I didn't worry, because she didn't really seem worried. She talked about getting a job as if it was something in the far-distant future, a kind of dream or notion or a worthy but unnecessary ambition. Meanwhile we were still in the little yellow house with its one picture-window eye, and every morning I ran out to play, and every day at noon I came home for my lettuce-and-mayonnaise sandwich, and every night we sat on the davenport and watched television until it went off the air. We were used to my father being gone. He hadn't left much of a gap in our lives at all.

The development was filled with kids, and new kids came all the time, and the tribe absorbed every one of them the way a stream absorbs raindrops. Even I had a friend. I'd met her the first day, when my parents sent me outside while they unloaded our furniture from the rented van.

There was an overcast sky that I could see all the way to where it met the horizon, straight as a ruler. In our yard the grass was still soggy and matted and the color of shredded wheat, but the trees were budding. They weren't the big old trees we'd had on our street in town, but new, young, skinny trees that had to be held up with wire, the wire in a piece of rubber hose where it went around the tree, so as not to cut the bark.

"Hey!" I heard. It was a girl yelling at me, another model of me in size and shape and even coloring. We faced off at the invisible fenceline between our yards like mimes meeting at an imaginary mirror. "Watch this," she said. I stood still and did as I was told. She went to her swing set, a rusty thing that pulled a leg out of the ground at the two peaks of her swinging. She pumped hard. Then, "Watch!" she cried, and let go, and went flying from the seat high into the air, coming down flat on her back a good fifteen feet away. Her head came down last, in slow motion, hair swirling beneath it. It took her a few minutes to catch the breath that had been knocked out of her. I was not disappointed.

Her name was Laura. Every morning that summer we met at our spot in the hills, which is what we called the place where the dump trucks dumped their loads at the outer edge of the development. Weeds and wildflowers and tall grass and brush leapt onto the mounds of dirt almost as soon as they appeared, so that some hills were sunken and hard and hairy with growth, others soft and sparse. I never thought about why this was. To me the hills had always been there and always would be. I had no idea they weren't planned to be a permanent piece of the landscape. The hills belonged to us, the dozens of kids old enough to be out on our own but not too old for dirt. We knew every inch of them. Beyond them was the open prairie, undulating like a golden sea.

In my and Laura's spot, a flat space in the crotch of three hills, we hid and buried objects of great value to us: two silver spoons from Laura's mother's velvet-lined box; a pink rubber douche bag; some matchbooks sealed in a babyfood jar; pieces of interestingly shaped wood we used for plates, paddles, or weapons; fragile baskets we made out of wheat straw. Most precious of all was a large, heavy egg that we shaped from mud and hardened in the sun and gave two stones for eyes. We called it "the baby."

When I got there that day, Laura was sitting Indian-style at the center of the rough circle where the grass had been worn away by our games. Out of the ground in front of her she had carved a shallow bowl, and into this bowl she had poured some water, making a mud paste. She beckoned to me, and I came and sat in front of her, folded my legs like hers, and closed my eyes. She began to paint my face and arms, her fingers wet with yellow mud sliding over my skin. We were Indians. We were at war. We were solemn. In a little while one of us might be killed, protecting our land, our food, our baby.

Next was the ritual of the stones. Laura dug up the matchbox they were in: two agates the size of sparrow's eggs. She put them in my hands, and I held them as she poured water over them from our douche-bag canteen. I liked agates because I imagined them to be the fossilized eyes of prehistoric creatures. Laura liked them because they were yellow and you could see through them.

The ritual was her idea. She had told me that it was how Indian women prepared for war. She had had to explain to me about sex, about rape. I was the new kid; I didn't wonder how she knew such things, I simply believed her. This knowledge of hers somehow came with the place. We squatted down facing each other, and Laura said, "May the ghosts of our ancestors bless this day, and keep us safe from our enemies, and make us strong," only in Indian language, and each of us pushed a cool stone up inside the loose leg of her shorts, up inside herself, into the private nameless place. And there the stones stayed as enemy arrows struck and penetrated the crumbling earth all around us. Two hills over, boys waged another kind of war, one with bombs and bullets; not far off a power saw sang to the rhythm of the construction of new houses where new children would soon live.

When the power saw was quiet, we knew it was time for lunch, and we slid the stones out, blessed and hid them, then made our way back, creeping through the brush, still Indians right up to Laura's house, where we washed off with the garden hose and she held it for me so I could drink the gamy earth-chilled water. Then Mama called me, and wordlessly I ran off, leaving Laura, in her dirty pink-checked shorts and matching shirt, holding the nozzle for herself.

I did not know he was home at first because as I came through the garage to the back door there was no car, as there had not been in the month he'd been gone. There was no car because the car had been wrecked. My father had almost been killed. This my mother told me as she and I sat at the kitchen table over our sandwiches. He was upstairs—sleeping, she said. His arm was in a cast, and his ribs were bandaged up. His face was bruised, his eyes black. He was thin and sallow— "like a Chinaman," she said. She was trying to get me to feel sorry for him. I did not. She was acting happy to see him again, glad he was back, and I could not understand why. I didn't know why we needed him.

I could not eat much of my lunch. As soon as she let me, I went back outside and off to the hills. I heard the power saw start up its whine again, and the erratic hammering. I went to a place where some boys had stockpiled old bottles and jars to practice slingshot on, and I picked up a Coke bottle and threw it at a pile of rocks. I smashed a dozen bottles to pieces, but still I wasn't satisfied. Then I heard a rumble, and the ground moved under my feet, and I ran to hide behind some tumbleweed. It was the gargantuan dump truck, its wheels taller than I was, its metal sides crusted with dirt and rust. The arm of the anonymous driver hung out the window of it, flicking a cigarette ash. This was the Neanderthal of trucks, and it made my father's sleek black car, now demolished, seem delicate and feminine, the same way the work the construction men did made my father's work seem unreal, unimportant. I didn't even know what he sold. I only knew that in the service he had not been a soldier, not like the ones in movies: he had only been a supply officer, and had never fought or even gone overseas. He was a man who did not know, really, how to do anything that mattered. That was the opinion I formed among the stones and broken glass.

As soon as the truck had gone back the way it came, I followed the deepened ruts it had left until I found the fresh mound of dirt, out at the edge of the hills, out where the prairie resumed, flat as a bedsheet. I picked up a lump of the moist soil and smelled it and broke it in my hand. There was an earthworm inside, elastic and squirming. I pulled it in two and threw the pieces back down.

When I came home for dinner that night, he was on the davenport, tucked next to the arm of it, small and sitting straight with a drink in his hand, rattling the glass so the ice clinked. He had on an open-necked, short-sleeve white shirt and some black pants, like an off-duty waiter; his feet were bare and white, and his arm in its cast was folded across his chest like a bird's wing. Mama was in the kitchen, making something to eat: I could hear her moving around and I could smell the smell of her cooking, but it didn't make me hungry. He looked at me without speaking for a moment, as if placing my face, and then he said, "Turn up the volume, would you, honey?" I went to the television and turned it up for him, and then I went to my room.

There was no fight that night, but I stayed awake anyway, watching through the crack in the door. And late that night I saw my father, walking down the hall to the bathroom. I couldn't remember ever having seen him naked before. And seeing him that way now, the cast across his concave chest that was roped with bandages and the hairless hanging thing Laura had described to me, I knew completely and certainly that I

8

did not love him, nor could I ever love him. He was too fragile to be loved as a father should be, the bones of his rib cage no stronger than the reeds that Laura and I snapped between two fingers to reveal their dry, hollow core.

In a few weeks Mama had brought him back to life. The bruises faded first, the ribs healed, and then at last the cast came off his arm. In celebration that night they went out, leaving me at Laura's. We played Monopoly on the living-room floor, bathed in television light. Laura's little brother, Jimmy, dogged us, wanting to be included. Since he was only five, we let him zoom the metal car around the board, his fat-cheeked face dimpled. At six the clock stuck out its tongue and the little bird opened its mouth and cuckooed, and Laura's father came in through the door, his tie loosened and briefcase in hand. Laura and Jimmy hurtled toward him, screeching with pleasure.

The table was made for four, but for me they added a fifth place, at an angle to everyone else's. We had pork chops, green beans, and mashed potatoes. Laura's father gnawed at his bones afterward and smeared the marrow from them on a piece of bread to eat. Laura's mother made me eat two servings of vanilla pudding. She said I looked thin.

Laura was allowed to stay up with me until I was "fetched." We sat curled up at either end of the davenport, our eyes drooping, trying to watch one of the variety shows. For a while her parents sat at the dining table and talked, looking over some papers her father'd brought home with him, but by the time my father came, they had joined us in the living room. My father's face was rosy and smiling, his breath smelled sweet, and he put his arm around me while he talked in his salesman's voice to Laura's parents, telling them about the accident and how good it was to be home. For a moment there, sleepy in the warm aura of his body, I forgot how much I had decided to hate him. Then I saw that Laura's father was looking at him as if he were some foreigner, and I slipped myself out from his grasp and into the dark yard, running.

Mama was already in bed. I went in and saw that she was

rosy too, and went to kiss her and smelled wine. She put her arms around me and called me "honey," instead of by name the way she usually did.

That night I heard the other kind of violence that my parents inflicted on each other, and I had evidence that what Laura had told me was true. I imagined my mother putting a stone inside herself to stop him from what he was trying to do. I imagined myself shooting an arrow through them both and into the bed. An image came to me—maybe it was a memory, I don't know—something I saw when I was very young, still in my crib, when we still lived in the one-room basement apartment of my grandparents' house. It was my father walking toward me, naked, that thing of his sticking straight out, and a pair of my mother's underpants hanging from it, and my mother looking at him, her head thrown back so that the red of her tongue showed, her breasts moving independently of each other and of her body, which was shaking with laughter.

For a week it was the way it had been when he first came back from the service, all happy. Except this time I was not in it. I kept myself out. Every day I met Laura in the hills and played as if nothing had happened, as if her life and mine were as alike as we were, with our thin brown arms and legs and long hair. Other kids sometimes thought we were sisters, and sometimes we pretended it was true, lying there among the weeds, the crowns of our skulls touching. "Can I come live with you?" I imagined asking her mother, and I imagined her mother saying nothing, only opening her arms to take me in to a bosom fragrant with the smell of baking.

Then one night my father opened the kitchen drawer where we kept things like rubber bands and matchbooks and a screwdriver. "Jesus," he said. "What did you think would happen?" It was dinnertime; my father, trying to help, had gone looking for a carrot peeler, but he didn't know where anything was. The drawer was full of bills, unopened and unpaid. "Did you think they'd just disappear if you hid them long enough?" Mama just looked at him and said, "What did *you* think? Did you think we stopped living just because you were gone?"

Speechless for once, he walked out of the room, and in a while a cab came and took him away.

A few days later he was back, this time with another new car. They fought again. He wanted to go back to work, to do what he knew how to do, he said. They needed the money, he said. She wanted him to get a job in town. "Why do we need such a fancy car?" she kept saying. "A salesman is only as good as his car," he said, over and over again. "Maybe you've got someone else to impress," she said. "Maybe some bitch who likes louses?"

"I bought you this house so you'd be happy," he said. "So be happy."

My mother had been paring potatoes, and was holding a knife. She stabbed it point down into the cutting board. My father looked at me. "Why don't you go outside?" he said.

I ran between them, out the door and into the garage. The car was there, black and shiny, the whitewall tires glowing in the dim light. It took up nearly the whole length of the garage. I tried the door, and it opened, and I climbed into the front seat and lay down and closed my eyes and smelled the new smell of it, the smell of leather and rubber and clean, refined metal and sparkling glass. I put my hand on the steering wheel. It felt warm. It was ridged so that my fingers fit it, making it easy to hold on to.

After a while I got out and took my bicycle and went over to one of the construction sites, where I sat for a long time in the sawdust, looking at the way the twilight fell through the framework of the house and into the fresh cellar hole next door to it. Someone had dropped an empty Newport cigarette box, and I picked it up and gathered some things into it: a couple of bent two-penny nails, some sawdust, a cigarette butt, a piece of cellophane. I put the box into the saddlebag of my bike and then I began to ride.

It was August. The cool night air sheathed my hot skin in moisture. I don't know what brought the other kids out— maybe the air itself. They seemed to come from nowhere: one moment Laura was beside me, and then more of them came, the playing cards sputtering over their bicycle spokes. Nobody said anything except to let out a howl or a hoot now and then, but before long the sound of our riding was itself almost deafening, there were so many of us. We rode the grid of streets, closing in on each rectangle of houses as if it were a kind of dull rotting fruit and we an invading horde of bees. Dogs loped beside us like huge silent birds. Parents came out into their driveways and sat in lawn chairs, watching us and talking to each other, the glowing points of their cigarettes punctuating the dark. Beyond the houses the purple curtain of twilight deepened. One by one the other faceless children drifted home, until I was alone again.

Mama's voice came as if from a great distance, even though I was just across the street sitting in the moonless dark on the neighbor's velvety lawn. I could see that the car was gone; I could see to the back wall of our empty garage. I watched her stand there, arms akimbo, looking right at me but unable to see. She went inside, and then she came back out again and began to walk down the sidewalk. I decided to follow her, staying on the grass far behind and silent. I thought she would circle the block and come back to our house, but instead she kept going straight, out into the hills.

She had a flashlight and shined it on the ground in front of her, following one of the many trails we kids had worn. Now and then she called to me, my name floating out ahead of her in pieces. Pretty soon I was close enough to hear that she was talking too, talking as if she knew that I was there and could hear her. "I can't do it, baby," she said. "I can't do it alone."

I was glad he was gone, but she wasn't. She was thinking she would have to work again. She was thinking she would have to pay the bills. She was thinking we'd have to give up the house. She was thinking how to get him back.

I thought about the day we went to pick him up at the airport, the day he came back from the war. How pretty she had looked, her hair tied back in the chiffon scarf, and how he had looked in his uniform, taller and, in some strange way, kinder. In the cab we gave him the present she'd bought out of her tips. It was the watch. "Twenty-one jewels," she told him. He held his wrist out to me so I could look at it. It looked like an ordinary watch to me; I couldn't see any jewels. I couldn't see anything remarkable at all.

When she stopped it seemed sudden to me. I hadn't realized how close I was—close enough to touch her. I didn't. I took small breaths so she wouldn't hear me, and waited.

She turned off the flashlight and dropped her hands to her sides and stood looking up. We were past the hills, standing in the waist-high grass of the prairie. The sky out there was black, pitch-black—except for thousands of stars. A little breeze blew toward us from the vast openness, carrying with it the scent of the fields. Insects made their noise. Mama gave a little shiver. "Beautiful," she said. "Beautiful." Her voice was a sigh.

Tears came to my eyes, as if something in me had just brimmed to overflowing. I reached out. "Mama," I said, and fell into her arms.

Stephen

Stephen used to say that a white bird flying in our direction was a good omen. Even at the time it seemed an ironic way to sanctify our crossing the country at seventy miles an hour on a superhighway, but somehow, when Stephen said it, it felt right. The car was a 1967 Volvo, a station wagon with no rust even though it was ten years old and seemed older, with its rounded instrument panel and leather pouch for holding maps. We kept our money in the glove compartment, in a jewelry box bound with a rubber band; in the glove compartment also was a jar containing ginseng root, which Stephen thought would help keep us awake when we drove at night. There was no radio or air conditioning, and since we were traveling in a July heat wave, sometimes when I got out of the car my T-shirt was so wet that it hung down to my thighs. On the other hand, one bright dawn in Minnesota we saw a vast field of giant sunflowers, faces to the sun like a throng of worshipers.

For me the trip was entirely a lark, of a kind I'd never gone off on before. I had no reason for going except to get out of the city and to be with Stephen, a friend's old friend I'd met a few weeks earlier. I'd sublet my apartment and borrowed a hundred dollars to put in the jewelry box, and gathered up my camping gear, such as it was: Sierra cup, borrowed aluminum-frame pack, sleeping bag, poncho, boots, and an old package of moleskin somebody'd forgotten in my bathroom. The night before we left, it was so hot in New York City that we had one of those famous blackouts that lead, as surely as war but maybe not as significantly, to a population boom. And the next morning our leaving seemed charmed, with no stoplights

14

and little traffic to slow us down, at least until we got to New Jersey.

Stephen had friends in Chicago (who were getting married) and some in Madison, Wisconsin, and from there he'd planned a trip that put us on the tourist trail: through South Dakota to the Badlands, Mount Rushmore, the Black Hills, then on to Yellowstone, the Grand Tetons, and down to Colorado. I remember that first night, arriving finally in a Chicago suburb, twitchy from the coffee I'd drunk after the ginseng didn't work and Stephen almost fell asleep at the wheel. From the sauna of the car we went into someone's overchilled basement and fell onto twin narrow beds, and it was the first night since we'd met that we didn't make love. In the morning we ascended the stairs like specters and opened a door to the bright activity of wedding preparations, strange women asking us our names and offering plates of French toast.

I don't remember the wedding. I remember watching a flashy display of midwestern lightning from the front lawn of that house, and then transferring ourselves to a steamy apartment in the city. On a tinny stereo there, I heard Bob Wills and the Texas Playboys for the first time ever; and for the first time ever I had an orgasm. We were making love on the sofa while Stephen's friends were at church; at the exact moment I came, I remember looking out the window and seeing a huge India-rubber plant, waving its leaves at me from where it sat on someone's fire escape.

Later, we walked down the street holding hands and talked wisely about how this euphoria of ours probably could not last.

In Madison our hosts had a dog, huge with white fur, that reacted to the heat by shedding a kind of animal snow in the corners of their apartment. Madison lies between two lakes that would like to be one, and the night it finally rained—which everyone thought would end the heat wave—the streets flooded and Stephen showed me how to drive in high water, how not to stall or get the brakes wet. We saw an MG filled to its windows with murky water, but we didn't try to drive down that street ourselves. After the rain, it was hotter than ever.

Two other things I remember: Stephen making guacamole with blue cheese and leaving the avocado pit in the bowl to keep the dip from discoloring; and a discussion we had about my inability to swim, an area in which I compared badly to Maura, the woman he'd been with for three years in Colorado. She was skilled, it seemed, in many ways I was not.

After that we were on our own, until Boulder.

Somewhere I have a picture of myself on that second leg of the trip, standing in front of a yellowish rock formation in a man's undershirt and jeans. My hair's short, my shoulders are tan and muscled, and there's something unfamiliar about my posture. I seem unaware of myself, casual, more self-assured than I feel now. Of course, I was posing for the camera, and for Stephen, who used to say that most people's problems are rooted in the failure of confidence. He would stand on the far bank of a creek and yell this wisdom to me as I tried to get up the nerve to cross a single-log bridge, as he had done. Half the time I ended up taking off my boots and socks and rolling up my pants and wading, hoping that I wouldn't fall and drown, my thirty-pound backpack holding me under the rushing stream. The times I did cross on the log, something powerful surged through me. Probably then I looked as I do in the photograph, like a woman who drives a pickup and digs her own ditches.

Stephen had never been to college, but he'd read a lot, and had ideas. So on our weeklong hike into Yellowstone backcountry, instead of packets of freeze-dried food we took lentils, rice, fermented bean curd, and Baggies of dried fruit and nuts. For dessert we had carob-and-honey bars and herbal tea. Our food took more time to cook and, because it was chewy, more time to eat if it didn't need cooking; but no matter how hungry we were, it filled us up. One of the results of this diet was regularity; every morning, before we set out, we each took a roll of toilet paper and, away from the campsite, dug a hole and squatted like animals to shit. Often we'd be in sight of each other, but I got so used to not caring if I saw Stephen, or if he saw me, that it seemed unnatural later, when we came out, to close myself into a stall to use the toilet. Other things, too, would seem unnatural: shaving my legs and under my arms, for one; colognes and deodorants, for another. We took one bottle of scentless, sudsless, biodegradable soap with us, which we used for dishes as well as hygiene. And yet I had none of my usual skin problems—no bumps, no rashes, no itching. Whether it was the change in diet, the clean water, or simply staying longer in my natural oil, I don't know.

Even though I'd never before gone on a trip purely for the pleasure of it, I had dreamed about it—but about beaches, restaurants, hotels, not about hiking with no destination through woods and fields, seeing no one else for days, and having nothing to tell you where you were except ambiguous trail signs and vague, almost incomprehensible topographical maps. We chose the trails we chose because of their descriptions in the guidebook—"vast meadows of wildflowers" and "open woods with clear walking"—or because the trail led to something we wanted to see, a lake or a particular view. The meadow trails were so infrequently used, and growth was so strong, that often they would not have been visible except for the colored flags stuck on posts, which had sometimes been knocked over by animals or storms, so that we had to guess which way to go. If you'd registered for the red trail, you had to follow it and by rights stay on it till you came to your campsite; this was to protect the backcountry from overuse.

Generally we followed the rules conscientiously, but one exhausted night—I had pulled a muscle in my calf and we both had blisters—we cheated and stopped early at a ranger's cabin. Since the windows had no locks, we could have slept inside, but something about that seemed wrong. So Stephen only climbed in to "borrow" two packets of instant hot chocolate, which was treat enough to make us feel decadent and pampered. During the night we scared ourselves, thinking that bears might come foraging, as they did at the more populous campgrounds below—we'd heard stories of them breaking ice chests in two—and we dragged our bedding up onto the porch. As always, we'd hung our food sack in a tree, tying one end of a rope to the bag and throwing the other over a branch to pull it up. In the morning, it was still there, but some animal had rummaged around the fire and found the empty cocoa packets, which it had clawed to shreds with expertise.

Except for those times when we found ourselves in an area known for bears and so sang and clapped to announce our presence, Stephen and I talked in half-whispers, if at all. Each of us had a thick paperback—mine was *Dune* and his *Even Cowgirls Get the Blues*—and we read a lot, switching for variety every couple of days. Setting up and breaking down camp became routine, requiring no discussion. Stephen kept a diary, which seemed all the listener he needed, and I took pictures. Physically I was entirely content: exhausted at night, refreshed in the morning, well fed, and more than adequately stimulated by what I was experiencing—a run across an open field during a thunderstorm, a sun-dried antler or the flattened grass of a moose bed, lovemaking in the orange tent, the changes in terrain, sky, and weather, and simply the novelty and challenge of being "outdoors," a word that lost meaning when there were no more doors to be out of.

But sometimes I wanted to ask Stephen what he was thinking about; out there he seemed more distant, when I had thought isolation would bring us closer. There could be closeness without words, I knew, and from experience with other men, I imagined that he might see my questions as demands or indications of mistrust. So I kept quiet and tried to accept his small gestures and the fact of the trip, and to forget about the past and the future.

One day, a plane surprised us, buzzing overhead; then we heard the voices of other hikers coming toward us. Civilization. We stopped, and Stephen talked to the hikers, his voice enthusiastic. The new hikers were a family, parents and two adolescent boys, going in just for the night wearing sneakers and carrying light packs. Obviously inexperienced. Stephen clearly liked seeing them and telling them about the trail they were taking, a short part of the longer trail we'd done. He even told them about the coyotes singing at dusk and dawn on the ridge. By the time we got back to the car I was ready to plan our next hike, but Stephen wanted to rest a few days, take a shower, eat in a restaurant, and sleep in the back of the car down among the "white man," as he called the tourists in their Winnebagos.

We did hike again, in the Wind River Range, but it wasn't the same. What did I expect? Nothing's ever the same the second time, ever as good, even when it should be better. Afterward we headed toward Boulder; I remember stopping in Rock Springs, Wyoming, and eating in a diner where all the music on the jukebox had Spanish titles. The incredibly tall and thin and weathered man who sat next to us at the counter told us that he was a prospector for a mining company, and for a hobby collected Indian arrowheads for his grandchildren. He said, "There's only two things that gets a man into trouble: whiskey and women. I can't do without whiskey, but I sure as hell can do without women."

From there the world began to seem gradually more familiar, traffic and supermarkets and cars, until finally, one weekday afternoon, we arrived in Boulder. In the apartment where we were staying with friends of Stephen's, I caught sight of myself in an unexpected mirror. I'd lost weight and my hair had grown and I was tan and healthy-looking; I looked like someone else altogether. While I was standing there, the phone rang; Stephen answered it. It was his old girlfriend, Maura, calling—just as surprised at hearing his voice on the line as he was at hearing hers.

A week later I found myself hitching a ride east with a friend of a friend of Stephen's, an overweight woman who smoked and listened to the same eight-track tape all the way across Kansas. She only let me drive once, for a couple of hours, and talked nervously in a thin voice that I had to strain to hear, though I hardly wanted to. We got into one of those midwestern thunderstorms, waves of rain and lightning that followed us for most of the night. She said she couldn't afford a motel, and I didn't want to prolong the drive, so we didn't stop. I was afraid that she'd fall asleep at the wheel, and so all night I stayed awake by telling myself the story of my trip: the driving, the hiking, the nights outdoors; then Boulder, and the drinking, and the crying. How Maura's news that day on the phone—that she was marrying someone else—had somehow cost me Stephen. How I had come all that way, only to fail. How on our last night, lying on the porch in sleeping bags, Stephen told me that, *because* he loved me, he had to let me go.

It was the first time anyone ever said that to me, and the last time I ever believed it.

Really Love Him

It was twenty degrees below zero and 3 A.M. on the second of January when the truck went up on us. I was with Larry, the bartender my friends were living with. He and I had ended up together after a New Year's Eve party at the bar, and I'd come back that night to keep him company. The bar was always dead on New Year's Day night, and Larry didn't know why they opened up. But even the owner was there, sitting on a stool by the door and smoking, wearing this cream-colored felt hat that made him look Italian, like something out of a movie.

Larry was tall—six-four, I guess—and attractive in an ugly way. He had a lot of scars, on his face as well as elsewhere. I'd seen a picture of him at eighteen, before he got involved in drug running, and I knew he used to be handsome in a pretty way, with soft eyes and smooth skin. Knowing that made him more attractive to me, maybe, than he would have been otherwise. Also the way he stood behind the bar—totally inappropriate to it, like a football player in a lingerie store or a brick inside a fish tank.

Larry had to clean up, so we left the bar late. When we went out to the parking lot, the owner was still inside, talking on the phone to some guy who'd been at the bar earlier and had since spun off the road into a ditch a few miles up. The guy wanted somebody to come pull his car out, and the owner of the bar had four-wheel drive and a winch. But as we walked out, he was saying, "Get a ride home and we'll go get it tomorrow. I'm dog tired."

Larry's truck was an old Ford with a Corvette engine he'd put in for more power. Just that morning he'd also transplanted a rebuilt starter, but on the way to work the truck had stalled and he'd had to run alongside pushing while I tried to pop it into gear. So I don't know why we expected to make it home. I was dressed for walking in the cold, but I hoped I wouldn't have to. I was dog tired too.

We had some trouble getting the engine to turn over—me hunched and shivering and him swearing and then grinning with relief—and then we were finally on our way. I remember I was thinking, Well, it's only a few miles, we'll make it, when we came to a hill, snow packed down on it until it was almost icy, and Larry put the truck into third gear and wound the engine up, accelerating as if trying to keep from sliding backward. The rear end of the truck was fishtailing, and I kept expecting to head into the ditch like the guy on the phone; that's easy enough to do in subzero temperatures, traction next to nothing and tires stiff from the cold. I kept looking at the trees going by, dark off the side of the road, thinking with each one we passed, We're okay, we're okay, we're okay. Then the engine made a high-pitched whine followed by a big crack, and we rolled to a stop not quite at the top of the hill.

We got out. "What happened?" I said, already sensing it was going to be a three-mile walk home.

"Blew her up," Larry said.

We walked back behind the truck. Along the road, leading up to us, was a trail of black oil, spattered like the engine's blood on the snow. "Shit," Larry said. He was angry at himself, and pretending to be worried about me making it home. But he was the one who had been drinking and wasn't really dressed for the weather. I didn't say anything, just let him tuck my scarf into the collar of my coat and pull my hat down over my ears. He kissed me on the nose. "We'll be all right when we start walking," he said. "Goddamn truck."

We started walking. The snow was hard, and slippery, and it sounded like Styrofoam under my boots. I was glad I had worn two pair of socks. We hardly spoke. We were in the middle of the country, there was no house before Larry's, and there were no streetlights, no moon. But it was a clear night—which was why it was so cold—and the snow itself gave off light, a cold reflection of the stars. After a while we warmed up. Larry's boots had less tread than mine, and one time he slipped and grabbed my arm. After that he kept his hand in my pocket, his arm linked with mine, as if he were holding me up.

I remember thinking that I'd never done anything like walking home that night. Once Larry got over what had happened to the truck, there was nothing but the white land, the dark air and trees, the sound of our feet moving down the hidden road. The land, the trees, the air, everything seemed to sleep a deep, deep sleep, almost like death, but more like a perfect sleep, a sleep without dreams. If we could sleep like that, we wouldn't wake up with pins and needles, deadweight hands, or stiff backs. Sleep like that would be comfortable. Yet you could wake up out of it, if you wanted—so it wouldn't be like death at all.

It was a long walk. By the time we saw the darker shadow of the driveway alongside the road, my nostrils were frozen tight and I was ready for bed. Inside, his face orange in the fireglow, Larry put more wood into the stove so that the house would be warm in the morning. (Years later, I heard about a fire that burned part of the house down, in the middle of the night, just after Larry got back from Turkey. Fortunately nobody was home. The fire ran up through the chimney and into the bedroom where I slept with him those nights. Larry had always been unlucky: one girlfriend of his had died in a car accident, another left him for his younger brother. And when he was nineteen he'd been arrested in Mexico; for him, that had been the start of it all.)

We went upstairs. My friends Lynelle and Albert were asleep in the other bedroom; they didn't like to go out much, I think because they were older than we were; between them, they had five teenage kids. They treated the kids like peers, to the point that when the kids visited—they all lived with their other parents—Lynelle and Albert would get them high. But Lynelle and Albert didn't particularly like bars or parties. They liked to stay home in front of the fire and play board games.

I knew Lynelle originally from work; she had been living in the city when I started my job at the station, and a couple of months later, when she moved to the country, we kept in touch even though we'd never really gotten to know each other well before then. So for a while I had been coming to visit her, always someplace different. I'd seen her through three affairs, but didn't make it to her and Albert's wedding. I liked Lynelle because she seemed so easygoing, but Albert was a mystery to me. He was always talking about setting me up with someone; even Larry might have been his idea, though I didn't like to think so. Maybe he was only joking when he talked about the four of us doing it in front of the fire, but however he thought of me, it didn't stop him from putting his hand between my legs when I was standing at the sink in the kitchen, or pushing himself against me while we were dancing, or coming into the bathroom without knocking when he knew I was in there. I laughed at him, hoping he would get the point. I didn't want to insult Lynelle by making a fuss about something that might be a joke.

I didn't want to make love with Larry that night after the truck broke down. I was tired and cold and I had a bus to catch in the morning, and I knew from the night before it wouldn't be much fun for me. We got into bed—the sheets were almost clammy—and I pulled the covers up around my face and turned away from him. I heard the light snap off and his jeans fall, the keys and wallet hitting the floor. He slept with his shirt on, the one he had been wearing all day. The bed sagged as he got in, and for a minute I thought he would just roll over and go to sleep himself. Then I felt his hands on my back, hard and cool, and he said, "Let's get warmed up, okay?" Later, he asked me if it had been all right, and I said yes. After a while I got some sleep.

The next morning when I came downstairs, Lynelle was fixing breakfast and Larry and Albert were outside fussing with Albert's car, a secondhand Mercedes he'd been abusing for a year. I could see Larry's black-and-red jacket, and Albert's round, blue-down self, huddled over the engine. "Won't it start?" I asked Lynelle. She had a bowl and a whisk in her hands; her hair was a blond-and-gray halo. She looked sleepy-eyed at me and said, "Don't worry. We'll get you to the bus in time."

"I'm not worried," I said, but I didn't want to spend another night with them. They were my friends, but I'd stayed with them past the limit before—before they'd moved in with Larry—and I knew how it could be. Albert got worse with time.

Before Lynelle and Albert moved in with Larry, they'd been living in the village, in Albert's studio; he was a sculptor. Then they'd moved out to help Larry finish his house. Living in the country had made them think about Lynelle having a baby of their own. But Lynelle was almost forty, and Albert almost fifty, so it was going to be risky. Still, they seemed to need it, or maybe they just wanted it badly. The other kids, Lynelle's two and Albert's three, had turned out mostly all right, considering that they'd been treated like grown-ups most of their lives.

Larry came back into the house and got himself some of the coffee Lynelle'd just finished brewing, and held the cup in his hands and blew into it. "Jesus," he said. "Is it ever cold out there."

"Where's Albert?" Lynelle asked.

"Gone over to Jake's on the snowmobile. The Benz needs new plugs."

"Christ."

Lynelle set the bowl full of beaten eggs down on the counter and went to the window. We all listened to the buzz of Albert's snowmobile fade away. Lynelle's reaction surprised me, since that was what Albert had always been like: it was just like him to forget about the spark plugs until someone had a bus to catch, and then take off without telling anyone. So I figured she was upset on my account.

While we were sitting waiting for Albert to come back for breakfast, we took some pictures. Larry wanted one of me, he said, and so I said I wanted one of him too. Lynelle got the Polaroid out, and Larry sat on a stool and pulled me onto his lap and hugged me tight. I smiled for the camera. The flashbulb flashed. Then I made Larry stand up by himself in the middle of the kitchen floor, in his checkered jacket and holding the cup of coffee. His hair was a mess from taking off his wool cap, and the collar of his shirt was tucked half into the jacket, half out. I took the camera from Lynelle and stood back a few more feet, and took one of him, head to toe.

25

Then we took more pictures: one of Lynelle and me mock-kissing, one of Larry and Lynelle in an embrace, one of Lynelle by the sink, her back to the camera, looking over her plaid shoulder. The pictures came out of the camera like tongues; we put them on the countertop and watched them develop. Then Larry looked at me with a smile and said, "I should get some shots of you upstairs," and Lynelle laughed and said, "Let me do the honors, and you both pose." I laughed but went down to the living room, sat on the daybed they were using for a couch, and picked the newspaper up off the floor. It was dated December 31 and had a red-and-green banner headline: NEW YEAR ARRIVES TOMORROW. In the margins were squiggles and trapezoids to represent streamers and confetti.

Well, Albert wasn't back. There was only one frame of film left, and Lynelle wanted to save that so I could take a picture of him when he did return, to remember this visit by. Lynelle whipped the eggs up again and started to make us breakfast. It was nearly time for me to leave, but by now I had guessed I wasn't going anywhere soon. I imagined that Albert had planned this whole thing to keep me around for Larry's night off, when we could all be home together for a long sit in front of the fire. But I went upstairs and packed my duffel bag anyway, just in case he got back in time.

At breakfast, Lynelle didn't seem mad anymore, but she wouldn't sit down to eat and started washing the dishes instead. Larry kept one hand on my knee under the table while he ate his eggs. I was thinking about the picture of him that was in the living room—the one where he was eighteen, young and clean, no scars—and I was thinking of the new pictures of him that were lying on the kitchen counter. Two women lost in as many years. And I didn't love him or even like him very much, and he knew it; he knew we were just pretending and that I couldn't wait to leave. We would never talk about it; that's what struck me as sad.

Noon and lunch came and went, and no Albert. Lynelle suddenly became calm and got out a piece of embroidery work she'd started a year before and had made a New Year's resolution to finish. She sat on a chair by the stove, her knees pressed together, her face serene, the piece of coarsely woven cloth in her lap. I could easily see her pregnant and having a baby to take care of at forty. She was a warm woman with a big heart, and I thought she loved Albert, although what they seemed to have in common wasn't much: drugs, kids, and being older than Larry and me and a number of their other friends. There was obviously more to it than that, but she had never told me what it was.

I'd missed the first bus of the day, but there was another at four. Still no Albert. I was beginning to worry about him, but Larry said, "He probably had to go into town for the plugs. Albert can take care of himself. He just doesn't like to use the phone." So I wasn't the only one worried. But we had no working vehicle, no way to go after Albert.

"Did you fill that thing with gas?" Lynelle asked Larry, meaning the snowmobile. She tried to make it sound like a joke.

"Sure," Larry said. "It was full."

Though we all worried, I don't believe any of us thought anything really bad would happen. I imagined Albert in a lot of situations: standing by the road hitchhiking into town, leaning on a car in a steamy garage, stopping on the ridge on the way home to smoke a joint. But I didn't imagine, for example, that he could have rolled the snowmobile over and was lying freezing to death in the snow, or anything terrible like that. I was—we all were—so wrapped up in being where we were, by the stove in the warm house, with the wind and snow locked outside, that we couldn't imagine anything horrible. Lynelle made hot chocolate and we sat around and listened to some music. Larry brought out his favorite board game—one with little plastic pigs you rolled like dice—and he and I played that for a while. Lynelle finished a big corner of her embroidery and held it up for me to see. "That's really nice," I said. I asked her what she was going to use it for.

"Well," she said, "when I started it, I was going to frame it and hang it over the mantel. But now I think it'll make a nice pillow for the baby's crib."

The embroidery was intricate, with tiny purple flowers, green leaves, and larger yellow flowers, and a border that made me think of filigree, all in glossy silk thread. She'd copied the

27

pattern from a Metropolitan Museum catalog. She had a talent for things like that. (A year or so later she called to tell me about the birth, about what happened to the baby. She'd lost a lot of blood, and it took a while for her to get well enough to start trying again. In the end, she and Albert gave up drugs so they could adopt.)

Larry turned on the TV. The reception was especially bad because of the weather—by now it was snowing hard—but we could hear the sound just well enough to tell that it was "The Bob Newhart Show." Larry taught us a game, getting out a big bottle of Black Velvet his boss had given him for Christmas. Every time someone on the show said, "Bob," we each took one good swallow out of the bottle, passing it around. "Hey Bob" got two. "Hi Bob" got three. And if anyone said, "Hi Howard," we had to down a shot, the way college students do tequila. By the end of the show we were all completely smashed, including Lynelle.

It was three o'clock in the afternoon. We lapsed into silence once the program was over, and Larry turned the TV off. We stared out at the snow blowing against the glass in white waves. I don't know what they were thinking about; I guessed Albert. I was thinking about my situation: visiting with people I was pretty sure I didn't like, drunk to the point of being sick, sleeping with a man I didn't feel anything for. I thought about how these visits really didn't seem to have anything to do with my life: after I left, I'd think about Lynelle once in a while, send her a card with a reproduction of some Dutch painter's flowers on it; I'd try not to think about Albert; Larry would call me a couple of times, but since I didn't live nearby and he wasn't made of money or in love with me, that would stop. Lynelle would drop me a line when she got pregnant. I'd go back to my regular life, my other life, which would seem safe and sane and real in contrast to this, and it would seem sensible never to make the trip to the country again. It would seem that my friend Lynelle's life was too hard to think about, much less watch. Then, after a couple of months of working and nothing but a movie on the weekend and the same people over and over, finally one day I'd be having lunch in the cafeteria— maybe I'd be taking the cellophane off a pastry—and I'd start to remember it, life in the woods with a pine fire burning and snow and bottles of Black Velvet waiting to be opened, and Lynelle thinking about doing something big, having a baby or building a house, and Albert, when he needed to, making one of his massive carvings and selling it for four or five hundred or a thousand dollars, which they would live off as long as they could. And Larry, keeping them both sheltered and warm. And what was so bad about that? In the end I'd give them a call, get on the bus again, visit one more time.

Albert finally came back, his face bright from the cold, red even under his big beard. Lynelle took one of his hands and felt for his pulse, and he pushed and pulled at her, acting pleased that she cared, and started to make his excuses: Jake hadn't had the plugs, they had to go downtown to look for some, ended up drinking a few beers and talking. Lynelle accepted what he said, but pointed out that it was too late for me to catch the four o'clock bus, which was at that moment probably leaving. Albert apologized, and I said I would just catch the bus the next morning; I had another day off anyway. And then Albert and Larry went out and got the car started and went to the village grocery and came back with V-8, Tabasco, vodka, and celery, and chicken breasts and some garlic: Bloody Marys and Indian food. Albert would "gourmet." Larry tuned the radio in to a not-bad station giving fair reception, and he and I stood up and danced together to Frank Sinatra, our sock feet on the flagstone floor in front of the stove, in the room that has since been destroyed by fire. Outside, the snow was still falling, and of course it looked fine from the warm, dry side of the big picture window. Larry was talking to me about maybe getting himself a dog, and for a moment, just a moment, I found myself thinking that if it could always be like this—dancing drunk to a crackling radio, snow noiselessly sweeping up to us through the dark, and Larry's voice murmuring to me and his body warm against me—then maybe I could love him, and stay.

Traveler

When I came in, four round-faced young men were having lunch at the back of the café, where a door opened onto a sun-filled patio with white iron tables and chairs. Three of the men wore ties. They all looked newly shaved; their faces were pink and taut, which made them seem young and earnest. The one without the tie was ruddier than the others, as if he spent more time outdoors. This one reminded me of my brother.

I was on the road again. I had no itinerary, except that ultimately I wanted to be home, with my family. Since they weren't expecting me, I could take all the time I wanted. It was late summer. Some of the trees along the roadside had already begun to change color, more the farther north I got. Fruit-and-vegetable stands punctuated the route, which took me along small roads I remembered traveling as a child, on family vacations. I'd even been at this café before; in fact, I'd spent several months in this town once, passing through between jobs. It had been winter then, and I'd worked at a local bar and made a lot of friends, but only a couple of names had stayed with me. I could have called on these people, but I wanted to be alone, I thought; I thought I wanted to be self-sufficient.

Still, the four young men interested me, in the way that good-looking strangers usually do. There was the ruddy one, the one without the tie; of the other three, one was very dark, one redheaded, and one slightly balding. They did not seem to be friends; the three in suits sat with their shoulders squared, as if they were in church. Only the ruddy one, the one in shirt sleeves, seemed relaxed, his elbows on the table. A leather portfolio sat on the floor next to the redhead; he leaned over, picked it up, and removed a manila file folder from it. The dark man leaned over to look at the contents; the other two continued to eat and talk as if nothing were happening. An aura hovered about the four of them; I could almost see it, a gray-blue haze of subdued drama. These men were in business; this was a business lunch, as you might expect. It was a Tuesday afternoon.

My waitress came, took my order, gave me more iced tea. As soon as she left, I reached into my bag and pulled out my notepad and pen. I'd learned that eating alone in restaurants invited unwelcome attention—waitresses rushing you, people staring at you or trying to talk to you. But I could deflect this if I seemed busy. So I usually brought a book or something to work on; today it was notes for a piece I was thinking about: an article, to be accompanied by photographs, about the graphics of plowed and planted fields, as viewed from a jet plane. On a recent flight over Texas, I'd seen miles and miles of flat green circles inside brown squares, brown circles inside gray squares, gray circles inside olive-drab squares. Although I knew it was due only to flat land, corporate farming, irrigation and roads, the sheer scale of it made it beautiful, and what is beautiful deserves an audience. I was going to try to make other people flying over Texas look down at the ground and be appreciative.

As I paused to think, the dark man got up and came toward me. I looked down at my notes, sure he was on his way to the bathroom, and not wanting to embarrass him or myself by staring. But he stopped at my table, stood next to me, and said, "Ellen," which is not my name. "Don't you remember me?" he said. "It's me, Anthony."

Of course I didn't recognize him. But clearly he thought he knew me. I wish I could say that I did what I did without thinking, but the truth is, in that split second before I nodded, I processed my options, among which was a new love affair, and decided to take the risk. He pulled a chair out from the table, turned it around and sat on it with his arms resting on the arch of the back. He was a handsome man in his early thirties. He talked to me, asking questions, telling me that he'd heard my work was going well, that he still followed art (that was how he put it: "I still follow art, you know"). It was odd,

I thought, that my shadow-self, the woman whose name he called me by, was also in my field; clearly, though, she was an artist and not a critic. My waitress came with the salad, and this Anthony half-rose, as if to go; but—again consciously—I stopped him, asked him what was happening in his life now.

"Oh," he said, "nothing exciting. I took over my father's business when he retired." What business is that? I wanted to ask, but of course I was supposed to know. "Why don't you join us?" he said, pointing to the other table. "I'm sure we can fit another place." He was talking more to the waitress than to me; from the way she looked at him, eager to please, I thought he must be a regular customer, maybe even owner or part owner of the café. In any case, she said, "Sure," and went off to fetch the necessary things. And in a moment I was pulling a chair up to a table of strangers and being introduced to them all as Ellen, with Anthony praising my paintings (ah!) but especially my prints (lithographs? etchings?). "Do you still have that stone you broke your foot on," he asked (lithographs, then), "when you thought you saw something staring at you through the studio window? Remember?"

Of course I would remember something like that. I was surprised I wasn't still limping. Anthony turned to the man who reminded me of my brother; his name was Sam (my brother's is John). "That was me at the window, coming to lure her out for some fun. She was so dedicated that she'd stay in that hole all night if she could, but I wouldn't let her."

"Paid off," Sam said. "Look where she is now."

Nearer, this Sam did not resemble my brother so much as he did the young pictures of my father, in particular one taken the day he shipped out for Korea. (Is it called "shipping out" even when you're flying?) I felt myself stirred by him in the way I was by certain men I knew were unobtainable: a kind of ache filled my chest, as if we had already had our love affair and were saying good-bye. He looked at me a long time, as if he knew what I was thinking, and immediately I began to contrive some way to let him know that I was attracted.

Meanwhile, Anthony was telling his business-suited friends (the redhead and the balding one both had names beginning with J; already I'd forgotten them) the story of "our" romance, which he recalled with such zest and detail that I began to be afraid I would be found out. How could he not know I was not Ellen? I asked him how long it'd been since we'd seen each other. "Let's see," he said, closing his eyes and leaning back. "I think it was—seventy-six? seventy-seven? It was when what's-their-names got married, and we were both invited to the wedding. We got drunk at the reception and ended up making out in the men's room. We were at it for at least half an hour before they caught us." Nearly ten years, then, long enough for memory to fade. But still, I must have looked almost exactly like this woman Ellen.

I had decided that Anthony was too Latin, too hot and romantic for me. Sam, reserved Sam, with his ruddy face, half-closed eyes, and sun-bleached hair—he was my type. (How well "my type" matches my father. My analyst says it's typical. I even imagined that Sam had a sailboat, and that before the afternoon was over he'd ask me to go out on the lake with him.) He sat watching, just watching me, as Anthony talked on, waxing heroic. The waitress brought a pitcher of beer and five glasses, and though the two Js protested, Sam poured for all of us; I had the feeling he'd ordered it in code, or magically. He and I were nearly catty-corner to each other, since the places had been shifted to accommodate me; he didn't smile, but continued to look at me with watery blue eyes. "Cheers," I said, lifting my glass toward him, and he lifted his a little. "Do you remember our toast?" Anthony said, lifting his glass too. I shook my head. For the first time he looked perplexed. "Simple," he said, and raised the glass a little higher, looking into my eyes. "It was 'To us and only us!' "

"Of course," I said.

It was midafternoon. I'd meant to make it to the mountains by dark, but it really didn't matter. I could stay the night here just as well; I knew a bed-and-breakfast on the edge of town. Still, I felt the urge to leave; things were getting out of hand. Should I just reveal myself, tell them who I was and wasn't? We'd have a good laugh, perhaps Sam would ask me to dinner, or at least we'd part friends. On the other hand, Anthony was looking at me with more and more affection; he might not take the revelation well. He clearly wanted me to stay, hinted that he was free for the evening. Jack and Joe, or John and James, or whatever their names were—the two Js were looking at their watches and saying they had to get back to "the office"; the leather portfolio reappeared, they stood, shook hands with Anthony and said something about getting back to him, waved to Sam as they headed off. I nibbled at my salad. The Gorgonzola dressing—what I'd come for—wasn't as good as I remembered.

"Well," Anthony said. "It's just the three of us."

I thought, Now's the time to tell them. Then Anthony started to beckon the waitress over, saying he was going to ask her about dessert, but Sam shook his head and frowned a little, and Anthony called, "Never mind," and she didn't come. I said, "Listen," but neither of them seemed to hear me; Sam just pushed himself away from the table, his eyes half-closed, and rocked on the back legs of the chair. Anthony watched him, as if waiting for instructions.

Suddenly I felt very uneasy, and just as suddenly I knew why: These two men knew that I was not Ellen; they might even know who I really was. Somehow, thinking I was the wise one, I had been the only one in the dark. They were smiling at each other, not at me. I stopped eating. I felt afraid; whatever they had in mind, I wasn't interested any longer, and it was time to be back in my car, and on the road.

"I've got to be going," I said, standing.

"So soon?" Anthony said, but he did not seem surprised or unhappy at the prospect.

"Pay the lady's bill," Sam said, "and I'll walk her to her car."

"That's all right," I said. I dropped a ten onto the table and began to back away. "It's been pleasant, thanks so much." I turned and began to walk toward the door, nearly bumping into the waitress on my way. "Is everything . . . ?" she began. "It's on the table," I said, and got around her. I heard chairs scraping back, and footsteps behind me; in a second I was at the door and out, and down the sidewalk. But when I looked back, there they were, following. For a second I didn't see my car where I had parked it and thought it had been towed away or stolen, which they could have arranged if they were mafiosi, which everyone knew the town was full of. But there

34

was the car; I was next to it; I had my key out; I heard a voice at my elbow.

"You really don't remember me, do you?" said Anthony.

"Or me?" said Sam.

They were smiling, almost laughing. I shook my head. The door came open and I got inside, locked it. Anthony made a gesture, twirling his hand to tell me to roll the window down, but I ignored him and started the car. Over the engine I thought I heard him say my name, my real name, and I looked at him again; he was laughing, they both were, and shaking their heads. I thought again, hesitated; maybe they did know me, maybe we were friends? But Anthony had stopped laughing; his look was contorted and dark, lips pulled back so that I could see his canines; he rattled the door handle while Sam stood off on the sidewalk keeping watch, his hands in his pockets and a tight, amphibian smile on his lips.

Now I recognized them.

I put the car in gear and drove off.

Life in the Tropics

*Once, when I was a teenager, I made myself a dress. Sleeveless, collar-*less, it had tucks across the bodice, so that over my breasts it was tight; below them it fell loose to my knees. I made it of upholstery fabric from the remnant table, grape bunches and flowers and Greek-looking leaves: green, blue, and purple on an eggshell background. I loved this dress. I wore it for years—was still wearing it when I got married, at twenty. The fabric lost its crisp finish and became soft, like an old handkerchief; the armholes, which I hadn't faced, curled under at the edges and later tore; I gained weight, and the bodice, which had always been snug, became a second skin. It was only because the fabric gave so much that the dress still fit; I had to have my husband zip it while I held my breath. I wanted to wear it during my pregnancy but couldn't. I don't remember what happened to it.

What makes me remember this dress is the heat, which I've been contemplating, unwisely; it's generally better not to pay much attention to it, even if it does make you feel like a fish moving through sugar water.

I woke up before dawn today because the cat flung herself across the room and onto the dresser. I knew that her next move was to knock down my glasses or my rosary or the wooden box that holds my earrings; I'd lost a pearl between the tiles before. She was hungry or else wanted to be let out; the only way to find out which was to get up and go downstairs with her. She trotted into the kitchen, and I sat with her while she ate some shredded chicken left from last night's supper. When I opened the door, she flew out.

The air was cool then, but still damp. The sky rode low,

striped with thin drab clouds; the street lay half in shadow, half lit by the sun over the horizon. No traffic sounds, just birds, and everything green seemed to hang as if wet and heavy. I stood and looked, the cool air on my face, and wished it would last. Then I went back to bed.

Two hours later I woke again, the fan whirling over my head, sun streaming into the room, and my skin coated with a thin sheath of moisture, as if I had just been born. My head throbbed, my throat ached, my back and neck cracked as I stretched, turned, and twisted on the hook of the day. I lay there a minute thinking about the heat and praying for a storm, not a hurricane, heaven forbid, but one of our thunderstorms, the kind that happens when the sun has boiled the water out of everything—the trees, the grass, the gutters, the air—so that it rises and cools into mountainous clouds, returning to us in an afternoon downfall, like a child coming home from school. Most Augusts this is the rule, a daily occurrence, so predictable that by two o'clock people make a point of being where they need or want to be, at work, or in a café with a view, or home with a book. Because when the storm hits, there's nothing you can do. The streets race with water. Automobiles are up to their doors in it. Brakes have no effect; carburetors die. An umbrella only acts as a lightning rod, with you as the ground wire. Better to be inside somewhere, or on a porch, watching the extravagance, than wandering like a blind dog in the torrents.

This past month, or six weeks now, we've had the humidity, we've had the heat, we've had the clouds, but we haven't had the storm. Rain when it comes mewls a few drops, and then passes by. The city shrubbery stays green, watered by sprinkler systems, but elsewhere the crops dry up and cattle threaten to die for lack of hay as much as for lack of water. Every day in the paper, new estimates of damage done; but every day the clouds pass over, like driven sheep.

So I get up, and think about the heat, and pray for rain, and an old dress comes to mind. I always wanted to duplicate that dress; I remember looking, every time I found a fabric store, for the cloth or something like it. Half my lifetime later I bought a silk dress with big roses on it and three pearl buttons at the neck, and, to match, low net shoes and earrings of ivory carved into little roses. A clumsy cleaner ruined that dress, put a wire hanger through the shoulders. For years I also searched for silk like that, anything like that; my husband was willing to pay someone to duplicate the dress, because I looked so good in it. But anyway I couldn't have worn silk today, in this heat; the perfect thing would be my homemade dress, light as a spider web, loose and cool.

A jug of cold coffee, a plate of sliced banana, the newspaper, and I take my station on the first-floor veranda of my house. I live on a corner on a side street, but the traffic of the boulevard is close enough to hear, and people pass by on their way to the grocery, which is to the left of me, or to the café, which is behind me, or to the Italian bar, which is two blocks straight ahead. Practically speaking, it's an ideal location. But it's also human nature, or I should say my nature, to want what I don't have: to me the ideal neighborhood is on the periphery of town, with palms instead of gray oaks, where you have a view other than your neighbor's porch strung with laundry. Like too many other people, I often wish that I could move there, to one of the little Victorian cottages caked with gingerbread and sliced by tall, narrow windows.

The people who pass by my house every morning are as familiar to me as family. The man with a pink face shiny as a balloon, on his way to get the paper, who wipes his forehead with a rag, nods, and says, "G'morning." A woman with a shiny black face, more like a star than a balloon, sharp edged, on her way back from the market, with milk and bread that I can see through the green web of her shopping bag. She doesn't see me, or at least seems not to; her eyes are shuttered against the heat. Two boys running down the center of the street, kicking an invisible soccer ball between them; they don't notice me either. A girl on a bicycle, dog trotting behind, tongue out; a black man with torn sleeves; an automobile, music. Morning at my corner.

The newspaper is full of the same news: the drought, the drought. Someone points out that the drought will make little difference in the marketplace, two cents here, three there; in short, only the farmers stand to lose. I don't know any farmers, but on Sundays I like to drive out to the fields green and stretching to the horizon, lazy and full under the sun, and the cattle under the trees; the fruits and vegetables at the fresh-air market, in round row upon row; during the haying, the smell of dry, cut hay, in huge spiraled bundles, like giant cinnamon rolls. But farming won't disappear if the farmers go under, because the land will be bought and made to pay; it's the farmers themselves, the men and women who bring us something we need—we city people who become so dull with our bars and cafés, our shops and automobiles, our precise employments so unlike the large, risky life of the farmer, loading fragrant sacks of feed into the back of his pickup.

I set down my paper, take off my glasses, stretch; my cat does the same in her spot by the door; and we go inside, where it is still cool from the night before. Eventually the house will heat up like a box in the sun, which is what it is, and we'll have to rely on the fans, two overhead and one at our feet, to move the steamy air into something like a breeze.

Often William, like the storms of normal years, comes in the afternoon, driving up in his car, rearview mirror strung with glass beads, or on his bicycle rattling over the shells in the yard, or walking, like any other passerby. He bangs the door with his fist, yells like a drunk when the bars shut down early—or sometimes he merely rings the doorbell and stands there like a delivery boy. The cat's afraid of him and slides across the checkerboard of the kitchen floor to get out the back way as William enters the front. Her fear began the day I invited him to a dinner party; he came straight from the swampy woods wearing boots, heavy boots that dropped biscuits of dried mud and echoed as he walked. To her, it must have sounded like Armageddon. She's not as brave as I am, poor thing. I look at her where she lies, sprawled out, along the foot of the door, and ask her what she thinks. Will we have company for lunch? The odds are in our favor; it's been since Tuesday.

The sky, through the gap in the curtains, is splotched again with clouds, but not rain clouds, only white wisps, not strong enough for anything. The sluggish air moves over my desk, where I work at the monthly accounts, adding, subtracting, noting figures in the big green book where I keep track of the years since I bought this place. Looking back, I can see just how much I spent for food one week in April five years ago, how much it cost to have the cat spayed, what I paid for the brimmed white hat I gave William for his birthday two years ago—a hat he wears, he says, on his boat in the evening. My house acts as port of call, but he lives on the boat; the few times I went there, we could not balance on that narrow bed— like making love on a diving board, acrobatic. So I imagine him on the boat, his face in the shadow of the hat brim, his feet on the rail; he's looking out to sea at what's left of the sun setting, at a sky the color of cobalt glass.

Income from my husband's properties, here; here, the expenses of my living. There, a small balance. Always enough to keep going.

The cat and I retire to the kitchen, hungry for lunch. She gets a handful of cereal in her bowl, and I have salad. My old refrigerator has frozen the lettuce again, but thawed under a spray of cool water, it will do. I don't think William's coming today, at least not for lunch. Sometimes in the evening I'll hear him whistling up the alleyway behind the house; sometimes late at night a pebble hits the window in my bedroom, and I go down to let him in. He can come and go as he pleases; he's young, and needs that freedom. It irritates my friends, when they come for dinner, to see the place set for him remain empty: they try to hold their tongues, but they believe I deserve better, more. I believe you get what you deserve.

And when he does come, we drag the mattress out onto the veranda, and drink wine and lie there and look at the sky and listen, and it is enough.

The clouds are thicker now, a little more hopeful. My neighbor across the street sticks her head out the door and calls to where I am eating on the veranda, "Does it look like rain?" "It looks like it," I call back, and she nods and goes inside to tell her husband. I soak a roll in the olive oil at the bottom of my bowl; it makes the bread taste like meat.

Electric air, greenish clouds, a hiss in the tops of the trees—

signs of a storm. With the sun under wraps, it's cooler already. But then, the sky has gone black like this many times this summer—and just as quickly come blue again, without a drop of rain.

My cat and I take siesta during the hottest part of the day, after lunch, when the house settles, becalmed by the heat. We stay downstairs and lie on the cot under the fan and listen to the sounds, which sometimes lull us to sleep but today keep me awake. Aimless cars and trucks approach and pass, a symphony of Doppler effects: hiss, roar, then the hiss in reverse, layer on layer. Toward the center of town someone is hammering erratically, endlessly; toward uptown someone is sanding a floor, or planing wood, or maybe only vaccuuming; birds screech and twitter. I can't stop listening. My phone rings once, twice, but stops before I can get to it; the cat rolls onto her back, exposing the white of her belly. Finally I get up.

Outside the sky is split into two unequal parts. Clouds have walled off the horizon, but overhead it's clear. It's a strange effect, the trees lit bright green against the dingy clouds, as if painted on a gray canvas or superimposed photographically. If I walked to the kitchen and looked out the back window, I would see another kind of weather completely. Neither can be trusted. But it's nearly four o'clock, and I decide it will not rain today.

So in a white shift and blue scarf I set out. The sidewalk burns through the thin soles of my sandals, hot wind eddies around my arms. Despite the frantic sound of it from inside my house, the city this afternoon is dull and slow. People have deserted us because of the heat, have gone to the mainland to visit relatives. The tourists won't come back for another month, and restaurants and souvenir shops are closed for vacation, their windows empty behind amber plastic. Only the poorer natives remain, working people, and people like me who have no place else to go, and people who, like William, prefer the city empty like this and don't mind the heat. The trees in the park are blurred, dim; an elephant trumpets once, far away, in the zoo. The swings and merry-go-rounds at the playground rest, not quite still. I look down; my toes are coated with silky dirt.

By the time I reach the wharf, the sun and the whole sky are hidden behind a dark screen that no longer can be called a cloud: it's too encompassing, too complete, a wall. A gust of wind pulls at the scarf around my neck. Boats of all sizes rock in the green water, people rush around securing lines and stowing buckets and ice chests and fishing gear. In William's slip, the boat is closed up—no one home. But I can't make it back now, not in time, so I crawl inside, snap the canvas shut behind me, and climb down to the cabin, where I prop myself up on his cot. It smells of him, that odd scent like vinegar and warm paper; I can smell his shirts from where they hang on hooks by the door. It's almost as if he's here, with me. In a moment, rain comes down in sheer curtains, so thick and fast the porthole is glazed with water; the hull rocks against the pier, and thunder cracks overhead.

In my neighborhood, I know, men and women and their children stand under the striped awnings, looking up at the heavens and down at the river running through the streets, and thank God. And my cat has taken her place on the windowsill, where she watches the sky, watches and waits for me. Eternally practical, she knows the storm will not last for long, that soon the black will be split with streaks of blue, and I will come home. All that's necessary, she thinks, is to wait. And here in the boat too, here in the boat the same.

The Surgeon

Unlike his fellows, the surgeon did not see the human body as an elegant machine. In fact, as the years went by, he became unable to look at anyone, human or animal, without picturing the complicated mess of those internal organs, nestled together like a jumble of skinned fruit in a bowl, slippery and sliding over one another, membrane against membrane. The connections seemed entirely too tenuous, the structure shabby, the entire thing makeshift, accidental, confused and confusing. And his ability to cut, alter, reconstruct it? Purely serendipitous.

So it was that, in the years before his wife became ill, he had all but stopped making love to her. In retrospect this seemed his greatest failing. She was a beautiful woman; after the cancer took her over, the bones of her face shone through her skin with the luminosity one expects in saints. She had large, dark eyes, and her hair, even in those last days, was long and abundant, auburn. He used to brush it for her, feeling her sway toward him as he pulled the bristles through—aware at every moment that hair was only protein, a chain of dead molecules.

He had once seen slow-motion film of a certain kind of slime mold, had watched as the individual one-celled animals climbed onto one another's backs, creating the forward motion of a single unit hell-bent on reproduction. This, the presenter had said, was the beginning of social order.

He was not the surgeon in his wife's case; the very prospect made his palms sweat. Instead he sat in the waiting room with other victims' families, a cross section of suffering humanity. In one corner, legs sprawling out, sat a hulking, florid, thin-haired man whose shirt buttoned tight across his belly and chest. Occasionally a tear seeped out of one of his narrow eyes, the left or the right, but never both, and flowed over the mound of his cheek, stalling on the short bristles of a day's growth of beard. Across the room, as if to balance him, an elegant woman sat poised and erect, long legs in sheer stockings crossed at the knee, magazine open on her lap and manicured hand perpetually aloft between sips of coffee. But even she was powerless, waiting, watching, listening, and when the doctor came into the room—stripped of his green operating gown and now white jacketed, like some pristine waiter—she looked up, shifted in her seat, and squared her shoulders as if to accept a blow.

But it was not her turn, nor the florid man's, nor any of the others'; this time it was the surgeon's. He sat with his wife's doctor on the vinyl couch, saw the doctor's lips move with the news, the muscles of his mouth and jaw shaping the words. The two men spoke clinically, surgeon to surgeon, in a way doctor and patient rarely speak—of options, dates, tumors, and mestastases. "It's ugly in there," the surgeon heard his wife's doctor say. He turned to see if anyone else was listening, but they all pretended not to be.

Afterward he went to dinner. He was aware, as he swallowed, of the progress of each bite of food through the pharynx; felt each wave of the peristaltic action of the esophagus. The food accumulated heavily in his stomach; he felt it, just below his belt, and when there was enough to keep him going a few more hours, he stopped eating. Eating, he realized, was not a pleasure anymore but simply consuming, ingesting—a mechanical act, a purely biologic need.

He looked around himself at the cafeteria where till then he had eaten so greedily despite the clever mediocrity of the food. Always he had been surrounded by admirers there: nurses, other doctors, patients, or the families of patients; even the women who worked in the cafeteria had asked his advice, looking up at him with trust. Tonight, however, he was alone. Overhead the light fixtures buzzed; behind the cash register the cashier, eyes downcast, filed her nails; next to him, a layer of dust coated the sill of the window, and each metal slat of the blinds.

He went to see his wife. Her room had a twilit quality. She lay absolutely, resolutely still in her bed, covers drawn up under arms that lay straight out, palms up. Tubes ran into her nostrils and into the soft crook of her elbow. She breathed evenly but slowly. Not even her eyelids moved.

But as he sat down in the single chair next to the bed, she sensed him there, and slowly the dark eyes opened. "What is it?" she said. "What is it?"

He took her home a few days later, canceling office hours, shifting responsibility to other surgeons, younger surgeons. His patients understood, of course. He stayed home with her, caring for her, keeping her clean, providing for her comfort, watching her progress—or rather the progress of the disease.

It took its time. More than six months. They watched the seasons change, and then in May they planted the garden. Where in the past she had done it alone, now she could work only ten, maybe fifteen minutes at a stretch, and then she sat in a lawn chair and directed him: "Hoe down that presumptuous weed, boy!" she'd say, gesturing regally; and laughing, he obeyed. So they amused each other. They came inside with sunburned faces and watched television late into the night, their heads cushioned side by side in fat pillows.

He wanted to make love to her again, at least once more—or rather, he felt he should. He knew it would not harm her; that wasn't the problem. He simply could not bring himself to it. He had long since stopped desiring her, and to pretend desire now seemed absurd—surely she would see through him—as well as impossible. In some way her cancer was to him the most attractive part of her: the honest wildness of it, the liveliness with which it grew, overtaking its territory like roses climbing a fragile trellis, thorny and blooming. But he could not make love to her cancer.

Their garden did well. The soil, black from a farmer's compost, was hidden under straw to keep the weeds down, and bright green rows striped the gold. But by August he had to carry her to see it, cradling her in his arms like an invalid. She *was* an invalid. He felt one hand behind his neck, the other on his chest. Of all the organs, by then only her hands and eyes still meant anything to him. They alone were not cold yet. When she touched him, when she looked at him . . . As they stood in the bright sun, he bent his face to hers and kissed her. "I do love you," he said, although he thought it was a lie, and she said, "I know."

He wanted her to take the blame. The cigarettes she smoked. The rich food she ate. The wine, the whiskey she drank. She had sprayed insecticide on the bushes without proper caution, had relished watching the fat caterpillars drop off. She had opened herself to decay. Yet he knew that, whatever the cause, she was not to blame.

She was too good. What had happened to that woman who had left him once for months, who had slept with other men, who had lied to him, who had kept secrets, who had been in and out of sanatoria? who had taunted him, gloated? who had sometimes hated him, and with good reason? For years they had carried on, energized by momentum alone. Who was she now to be good, forgiving, to fill him with guilt?

One night, he dreamed they were young again. In the dream they sat in a sunlit room, reading. She was on the couch, her feet curled under her, he in a chair with the window light tumbling over his shoulder onto the page. As he read (he saw the words clearly, passing before his eyes, like a dream within a dream), he felt a strange surge—not of love or desire but of comfort. He was comforted there, with her; without looking at her, or speaking to her, or touching her, he felt in her presence a consolation.

When he woke from the dream, he reached for her, touched her shoulder, turned her toward him, stroked her breast, pulled himself onto her. "No," she said.

"Why not?" he said, letting his voice rise. "Why the hell not?"

Even then, angry as they were, they could not fight. She fell asleep in his arms.

Before much longer, she died. The surgeon returned to work. Women came to him with sympathy in their eyes, as yet unaware of the cancer in their own bodies.

The Housesitter

During graduate school I was resident advisor in one of the freshman
dorms, where I barricaded myself inside a wall of books that
would've been dangerous if the fault line running through
town had been active. Although in the interview I'd made a
good case to the contrary, I took the job not out of any altru-
istic notion of helping young men through their first year but
simply for the deal on room and board. In return for celibacy,
late-night rousings by drunken boys, and tedious R.A. pro-
cedural meetings on the first Monday of every month, I got
hot showers, colorless food in the pink-walled cafeteria, and a
tiny, overheated room, with no bookshelves to speak of and a
bed so small I slept on it curled like an animal. We're talking
about my early thirties, which in youth I'd imagined as the
age when comfort and luxury began. So you can imagine
how inviting the idea of housesitting must have seemed after
months of cramped quarters and aesthetic exile.

Dr. S gave me my first break when he and his wife decided
one June to follow Hemingway's footsteps into Africa. My
gratitude at being out of the dorm and into their Victorian was
so great that I went well beyond the call of duty (feed the dogs,
mow the lawn, water the plants) to repair the toilet, shampoo
the carpets, defrost the freezer, trim the hedges, weed the
flower beds, and perform myriad other small chores. And
when the S's came home to a clean house, a refrigerator
stocked with fresh essentials, their mail sorted, and the liquor
cabinet intact, they recommended me to Dr. Y, who was
about to go off on an intensive in Colorado; she mentioned me
to Dr. K, planning the annual visit to his mother in Maine;
Dr. K passed the word to Dr. Z, headed to the Bahamas for

47

Christmas. With no overhead and word-of-mouth advertising through the intricate network of academia, my only cost was food, and sometimes a bit of gas into whatever car I borrowed to move my books from place to place. It was the perfect summer and Christmas-break job for me, and in many ways I was perfect for it.

The key to my success was simple: I did for my hosts what they hated to do for themselves. Often lurking behind procrastination were emotions that loaded a job with personal baggage and made it nigh on impossible to conquer. For instance, as long as a broken cellar step symbolized her husband's lack of consideration, Mrs. M wouldn't have it repaired; as long as to Dr. M it signified her attempts to dominate him, he wouldn't fix it himself. To me, however, the broken step was simply a broken step, repaired in ten minutes with no under- or overtones. Besides, it's much easier to take charge of someone else's life for a short time than to be that person faced with limitless details needing attention endlessly. In fact, I enjoyed both the foreignness and the temporariness of other people's houses and things, and even the dirtiest chore—cleaning the garage or attic or the drainage gutters—held charm for me.

Housesitting evolved into a demicareer, my personal science. I developed theories, procedures. My approach was to adopt, as much as I could, the habits, tastes, and attitudes of my hosts, as gleaned from their decor, books, records, food, etc.—the theory being that a house, like a car or a human body, suffers under erratic driving, and so the ideal housesitter should slip in unnoticed, bringing as few changes with him as possible. I played Mozart if that's what was in the piano bench, cooked Chinese if the cupboard was stocked with black mushrooms and woks, rose at dawn if that's when the alarm was set to go off. It made for a certain harmony and let me try on different lifestyles, much as my ex-wife, Julia, used to change her clothes to change her mood.

All went fine until the summer before my comprehensive exams, which I was to take in October. My reputation, as an expert who loved living things and left his campsite cleaner than he found it, was well established: many weary travelers had come home to find an orderly house, thriving plants and pets, and milk, juice, and muffins in the refrigerator for their breakfast. So till then I'd never had to make an effort to find a position. But that year in May I still had nothing lined up for the summer, the crucial summer of study before the comps. Maybe it was the climate of the times: unrest in academia, a new president under the cupola, economic stress—whatever, people weren't traveling. It looked as if I'd have to stay in the dorm—as undercooled in summer as it was overheated in winter.

I rebelled at the idea, and for the first time did some advertising, in the school paper and on the bulletin boards. Finally, one night I got a call: a young couple was going out of town for the whole summer; did I have references? was I available? I pretended to check my calendar; yes, maybe I could manage it. Then I got on my bike and pedaled over to an address just outside the wall of big houses around the university, and met and talked with the Gs, Martin and Doris.

Martin was a graduate student himself, in classics, and Doris had worked, until that week, as a secretary in the biology department; they didn't have much money, but their rental house had "character," as real-estate ads say, which translated here to stained glass over the door, carved fireplace mantels, a staircase that was almost spiral. The mismatched furnishings—some Danish modern, some Edwardian, an Oriental rug—had obviously been collected over time. They didn't have much, just enough, three or four pieces in each big room, but I liked that; after the clutter of my nook, and thinking about three hot months in it, maybe I liked it more than I would have otherwise.

As for the people themselves, they were likable, too, from what I could tell. Martin was thin, with a vague, persistent smile; Doris was pretty in an equally vague way and about five-months pregnant. They planned to spend the summer and most of their savings traveling, and then they were going to visit her parents, who were, I gathered, well-off and lived on the shore in Maine. A second honeymoon before the baby came. Obviously in love, they even held hands while they talked to me. I showed them my references; they showed me the cat; the deal was struck.

HERE

By this time part of my service was to ask my hosts for a list of work they'd like done, but when I offered this to the Gs, they acted surprised, as if I was already doing them too big a favor just by moving in. They didn't want me to think of anything but the ferns and the cat; they'd even hired a kid to mow the lawn. So, after I'd seen them off a couple of weeks later, I took a tour of the house to see what needed doing; to me, it was part of the job, no matter how they felt, and I knew they'd appreciate it when they got back from so long a trip. Besides, I was curious. So I prowled around, opening closets and cupboards and drawers, looking at floors, walls, ceilings, window frames, and doorjambs, and generally being a snoop.

Upstairs, off one of the bedrooms, I found a sort of attic in which baby supplies were arranged as if on display; some were secondhand, like the stroller, but most were new and still in plastic or boxes: a playpen, little T-shirts, diapers, a crib, booties, hats with strings to tie them on. Everything was blue, so unless they believed in wishful thinking, they knew what they were getting—oh, the perils of science! A mobile of fish and birds hung in the middle of the room, moving around in the breeze from behind me—as if fish could fly and birds swim. This was one kid, anyway, who was going to get an interesting education. After a minute I closed the door and moved on, making notes on my yellow pad, thinking that maybe later I'd put the crib together for them, an idea which made me feel a little sentimental, even though I'd never wanted children myself.

Three months is a long time to be alone in someone else's house, or anywhere for that matter, but alone I was and had to be. My friends—the few I had—had either finished the program long before and gotten jobs somewhere while they worked on their dissertations, or were gone for the summer. But even if they'd been around, I'd have had to be alone in order to concentrate. Ironically, the reason I'd come back to school so late in life was to save my marriage. Julia had issued an ultimatum: either I did "something" with myself or she'd leave me. And I didn't know what to do but go back to school. Then, after we got there and she found out what life as a student spouse was like, she'd decided it would be better if she went off to do "something" with her life too. We talked sometimes about getting back together; so far it hadn't happened. Now that school was petering out, I wasn't at all sure I'd done the right something, but it was clear that I'd done it for the wrong reasons.

Studying for comps in literature overwhelms most people, and for someone like me, a lazy scholar at best, it's murder. You've got three area exams and one in a major figure or genre; even if you're smart enough to choose your topics so that they overlap and complement one another, the primary works could take years to read, much less study, and then there's the secondary material. I'd spent my first four years just finding what I needed, and buying, Xeroxing, or stealing it. Now I had the stuff, in neat stacks in the baby's room (I didn't want to clutter the house). And it was like approaching the maw of the whale every time I went up there to bring a new batch down.

I designed a program—four hours on and two off (for my eyes, which have a tendency to strain), with eight hours of sleep a night—and set myself up at Martin's desk in the dining room. Surprisingly, since procrastination is my biggest hobby, everything went well the first week; I kept to the schedule, and for the first time in years I felt better about my chances.

During the off hours, I ate and wandered around the Gs' house, spackling and painting over nail holes, oiling the wooden floors, getting to know Martin and Doris. By the end of the first week I'd read the poetry Martin'd written, perused the bookshelves, eaten their food, sat on their chairs, played the tapes they'd left behind, and listened to the radio stations they'd programmed into the stereo. I'd also looked at their photograph albums, slept in their bed, used their washer and dryer, and figured out their different methods of organization: he alphabetized books according to author and coded clothes by color; she categorized everything (bowls here, saucepans there, sweaters in this drawer, fiction on that shelf). I leafed through the used pages of the calendar to see what kinds of appointments they'd had, when their birthdays were. Contrary to my first impression, the house had its own kind of

clutter, things stuck in places you wouldn't ordinarily notice:
a clay cat peering over the top of a cabinet in the bathroom,
animal masks hanging from hooks in corners, a box of mineral
samples sitting on the mantel. In addition to bits of Greek pot-
tery, Martin collected what seemed to be voodoo charm dolls;
I knew they were his because, in addition to the ones hanging
from odd nails here and there, he had a bunch in his desk
drawer.

And in shelves they must have built themselves they had
books, hundreds upon hundreds of books. But still the house
felt calm, not frantic the way my room did sometimes, when
I lay back on my bed and looked at the teetering mounds of
literature around me. I found it easy to concentrate at the Gs',
as if each book were the last in the world, as if there were
nothing competing for my attention.

Studying for the comps, of course, was my first concern,
so to make it tolerable, I imagined it wasn't me studying at all
but Martin, who had somehow switched from classics to
American lit. Sometimes I even had lengthy imaginary conversations with Doris, summarizing for her edification the
themes of "Bartleby the Scrivener," the philosophy of Tho-
reau, or Leslie Fiedler's theories about Huckleberry Finn. It did
help, and so did my decision to tackle the authors alphabeti-
cally, the way Martin would, each one with the appropriate
secondary reading. For my notes I got loose-leaf binders like
the ones I found in his desk, and I became more organized
than ever.

In other ways as well I tried to adopt habits of the Gs.
Vegetarian cookbooks dominated their collection, so I became
vegetarian. There was no alarm clock, so I let the sun wake me
up, assuming that's what they did. When insomnia (due to
stress, I thought) started to bother me, I read from the book
Martin'd left open by his side of the bed—it was a French nature novel, very slowgoing. (I figured it was Martin's because
on the other side were "name your baby" and breast-feeding
manuals.) Martin had mentioned to me that the park nearby
was a good place to sit and read, so sometimes I headed over
there with a book—which never got opened, so distracted
was I by the women jogging past. But this and a thousand

other small things—like buying their brands of toilet paper and coffee—gave me the vicarious pleasure of living someone else's life.

After about a month my stamina had increased to the point that I could study for six hours at a stretch, with only an hour off between sessions. My eyes never felt strained, something I attributed to the better lighting at Martin's desk. And my back, which had always ached after a couple of hours sitting (I'd been in a car accident when I was eighteen), didn't bother me in Martin's chair, even though it was straight-backed and wooden. When I thought to wonder why things were going better for me, I knocked wood and told myself not to look a gift horse in the mouth. I needed all the help, and luck, I could get.

Then one evening I went out to start Martin's car, a '68 Chevy convertible that he'd clearly had for years. It wasn't much good for long-distance trips, so they'd taken the newer car and left this one in the garage, with lengthy, specific instructions as to how and when to start it so the battery wouldn't die and the engine would stay lubricated. It was my only chore aside from the cat and plants, and it was the only thing about being there that I didn't enjoy—something about sitting in that damp garage, staring at the bare planks of the wall, smelling exhaust. So I'd let more than a week go by since the last time I'd started it, and as I put down my book and went outside with the keys, I felt guilty.

It was one of those summer days, long on light and green, about eight in the evening. The garage seemed more damp and murky than ever, so I decided to go for a spin, which Martin had said would be a good idea once or twice, to rotate the tires. As soon as I started the engine—which turned over immediately—I felt strange, sort of queasy. I thought it might be because it had been so long since I'd driven a car. I backed down the driveway and into the quiet street, pulled out under the twilit sky, and cruised down to the main drag in front of the university. A few students were out, walking downtown; a train whistle blew, and the light I was idling at turned green. Somehow this confluence of details started me remembering a girl, her face and her voice; we were sitting on a sofa on the front porch of her house; the sofa was musty from being out-side, the girl's perfume was Lily of the Valley. A man passed by on the sidewalk in front of us, but we didn't pay any atten-tion, and a light went on inside the house, making a yellow rectangle on the narrow floorboards of the porch; we heard voices, and pulled ourselves apart. The girl's name, I remem-bered, was Sarah.

When I realized what was happening, I pulled over and parked the car. The memory was still with me, in me, and it was a lovely memory, with all the intensity of teenage love, of newness and sensuality. I wished it were mine. But it wasn't. Because, also in the memory, parked by the curb in front of the girl's house, was a car—Martin's car, this car, the car I'd been driving and was now sitting in, stunned by what I now realized.

The memory was Martin's.

Things began to click. That morning I'd put on an old pair of Martin's running shoes and gone jogging for an hour in the park—something I'd never done or thought of doing before, something neither Martin nor Doris had mentioned, though clearly (the shoes were well worn) Martin was an inveterate jogger. Later, sitting at the desk working, I'd noticed that I was holding the book closer to my face than usual because when I held it at the normal distance, the text was blurry; when I took off my reading glasses, I could see it fine—even though I'd always been farsighted, not nearsighted. Was I haunted, or possessed? Had I crossed a line somewhere, had I taken pretending to be Martin too seriously? Maybe every-thing—my new study and eating habits, my conversations with the imaginary Doris—maybe all of it was Martin, and not me.

I sat there for a long time. Then I took the car home, got my bike, and rode to the nearest bar, where I proceeded to get drunk. If I was going to be out of control of myself, I might as well go all the way. But everywhere I looked, some-thing—the college girls leaning against the bar, the pinball machine, the names carved in the old table—reminded me of something, something Martin remembered, not I. When I finally tottered home at closing time, I was so afraid to stay inside the house that I brought out a blanket and lay in the hammock on the porch, swaying and having dreams I couldn't be sure were mine, and waking up every so often, trying to remember who and where I was.

In the morning I felt sheepish. After all, I had no proof, and reasonable explanations were easy to find: eyesight changes as you get older, jogging is not so impossibly difficult, maybe I had known a girl named Sarah, or maybe someone had told me about her, or maybe all that reading was getting to me and I was having a hard time separating fact from fiction. It could all be attributed to an overtired imagination. So I went inside, cleaned up (was my hairline growing back in? or had I just exaggerated how much hair I'd really lost?), had breakfast, and went to Martin's desk to work, taking out the notes I'd been making the day before. I stared at them a moment before it sank in and I went to get a note Martin had written me and stuck on the fridge with a magnet. It was true: my handwriting had changed, from my usual right-slanting scrawl (I looked at the first notes I'd taken) to a neater, more upright script—a script almost identical to Martin's.

All right then. I'd put on Martin's hat, was filling his shoes, had taken his place—whatever metaphor you liked: I'd become Martin. It was the logical, if unbelievable, outcome of my experimentation. Somehow my willingness to give up my own habits for those of strangers had left me open to this. I didn't blame Martin; no doubt he had no idea what was going on. I blamed myself, for being weak willed and vacant, like a pitcher waiting to be filled.

On the other hand, as Martin, I was a better scholar. As Martin, I was eating healthy foods and getting more exercise. As Martin, I had Doris to talk to and pleasant memories of youth. As Martin, I was a better person all round, except for the insomnia. I felt and looked better than I had in years. My eyesight had improved, and my handwriting was more legible. As I looked over my notes, I saw that they were insightful, concise, and exactly what I needed for that last month of intense study before the tests. Better to be Martin, I thought, and pass the comps, than to be myself and fail them.

So I accepted Martin's life. Every day at dawn I rose, put on the running shoes, and ran. A quick shower, and down to work. Lunch at noon, and back to work. Dinner at six, talks with Doris, chores. Work till midnight, a chapter of the French novel, and restless sleep till dawn. And a pervasive, new sense of purpose, of interest, of direction, of single-mindedness. I actually enjoyed what I was doing—no, it was more than that. For the first time in my life, I was happy.

If I'd completely become Martin, things would have gone on like this, I think, till the end. They might be going on still. But my own personality remained—subdued, relegated to the background, but definitely there. And as usual I wasn't satisfied, not even with bliss. One discomfiting problem remained, and I wanted to resolve even that: the insomnia. As Martin, I didn't get much sleep, and each night I got less and less, until finally I could snatch only a couple of hours before dawn. It was then that I got the bright idea to sleep on the other side of the bed.

It worked. That first night, I still had the urge to read a little, but then Helen, the cat, got onto the bed with me and insisted that I put the book down and massage her ears, which is what I was doing, I guess, when I fell asleep. I slept straight through until dawn. After that, around ten in the evening Helen came and stared at me, as if asking why I needed to stay up so late; I found myself looking forward to going to bed, and then going to bed earlier and earlier, till I was getting a good ten hours every night, Helen and I curled up side by side on top of the sheet.

By August I was far enough ahead in my studies that when I felt the urge to take a break for a couple of days, I didn't worry about it. "Taking a break" meant cleaning house, cooking—black-bean soup, eggplant casseroles—and long walks in the park. I couldn't sit still for long, partly because I'd developed a twinge in my lower back. My two-day break grew into three, four days, nearly a week, and still I was unconcerned. Then one night I woke from a nightmarish dream—something about a roll-away truck—to find myself sitting on the floor of the baby's room, crying, some soft little piece of blue clothing in my hands.

I'd forgotten about Doris.

I suppose it was male pride that had kept the idea of my "becoming" Doris out of my mind; until that moment, it had never occurred to me that if I could absorb Martin, I could absorb her too. But there I was. I looked at myself: hips riding forward, belly slightly enlarged, as if I'd been drinking beer every night; my feet and hands were swollen; the veins on the backs of my legs bulged. I hesitated to look in the bathroom mirror, afraid of what I might see: I still needed shaving, but was my beard as thick as it used to be? Weren't my eyes changing shape, turning a deeper blue? Weren't my breasts enlarged? Had my penis actually shrunk?

How much of this was true I couldn't tell then and I can't tell now. But it was enough to frighten me thoroughly. That night I stayed awake, sitting at the kitchen table drinking coffee (something Doris would never have done, because of the baby), and thinking. By morning I had a plan. I had to fight, if for no other reason than because being Doris would ensure my failing the comps—not because she wasn't intelligent but because her interests were those of a nesting bird, not of a warrior preparing for battle. I cursed both of them for playing such traditional roles. If they hadn't, the whole mess might never have happened.

I found an old camping cot in the attic and set it up near Martin's desk, and from then on that's where I slept. I borrowed his clothes, and wore the jogging shoes constantly. I tested chairs to find out which ones made my back hurt— those had to be Doris's favorites—and I avoided them. Despite my limited summer budget, I began to eat out again at old haunts, fast-food places and diners, not even daring to risk cooking in the Gs' kitchen or eating off their plates. I thought masculine thoughts, and masturbated daily. I thanked God that most of the writers in the American canon were still male.

Yet at times I felt myself drifting, like a life raft cut free from its ship. Tears welled up in my eyes, and my focus became internal and vague. On occasion I even thought I felt movement inside me. One night I woke to find Helen perched on my stomach—the cot made me lie on my back, since there wasn't room to curl up—and I almost killed her, throwing her off in fear.

In moments like those it took all the willpower I had to turn my mind and body elsewhere. Sometimes I hid in Martin's closet, absorbing his scent; sometimes I went out to the car. After a while, Martin came back to me and Doris was vanquished—for the moment.

In my less panicked, more lucid moments, I tried to observe, to set myself outside both of them, to learn from what I experienced. I noticed that one sensation, and one only, seemed common to these two people: the feeling of expectation, of waiting for the birth. Because both of them felt it, I felt it all the time, and all the more strongly. It was going to be damn hard to leave before the baby was born, but then I was afraid to stay, afraid of what seeing them again might do to me. When Doris and Martin came back, who—or what— would be left for me?

I lost track of the days, or maybe I didn't, maybe my unconscious took over and made me ignore the passing of time. In any case, about dinnertime one evening, I was sitting at Martin's desk when I heard voices on the porch, a key in the door. My first impulse was to hide, but I couldn't convince my body to move; I got panicky, my hands started to sweat, my heartbeat pulsed so loud in my ears it seemed to be in the walls of the house. As they came in, I forced myself to turn, to look at them, to smile.

But as I did, everything dissolved in white light, as if I were looking into the sun. I couldn't see them, but they were there. I thought, I'm passing out. Images invaded my mind, a collage of scenes—other places, other people, the smell of bodies, the sensation of orgasm. Then, from somewhere in the distance, I heard a voice, saying my name, saying, "Thomas, Thomas? Are you all right?"

And suddenly I was, and I stood up, and said hello.

One evening two months later, we celebrated together, the Gs and I, eating dinner at their rickety table, the baby in his cradle nearby, my books packed away in boxes and loaded into the back of a U-Haul, the autumn leaves lying on the ground. "May I have your luck!" Martin said to me, raising his glass in a toast: I'd passed the comps roundly, and was off to join Julia in California. And I? Raising my glass toward Doris and then their sleeping newborn child, I said, "And I yours."

The Sound

We arrived late at night, and at first it seemed to me that I'd never been anywhere so quiet. Once the rattle of our luggage and talk died down, silence seemed to take over. We kissed good-night and were taken to our rooms, Richard to the east wing, I to the west. No one else stirred, and the long hall was like a forest corridor lit by the half-moon. The man who led me—I learned later it was Emmanuel, the butler—had a flashlight, which he shone ahead of us on the figured carpet, and then on the door of my room, number 32. He ushered me inside and efficiently set down my small bags, opened a window, turned down the covers. And then he was gone, I was alone.

I walked to the French doors, opened them, stepped out onto a small porch, and faced the lake, which I knew from the brochures must be there, but which, at that hour, was nothing but part of a great, endless stretch of black beginning at my feet. Because the night was overcast, there were no stars, no way to tell where land or water ended and sky began. And the silence. But as I stood there, the air began to fill with sounds, and I picked them out, one by one: first the lapping of water on the shore, some yards away; then the hum and click of insects, most likely katydids; an occasional animal call, a bird or dog, or something doglike; and finally an almost inaudible, unidentifiable sound—a low, continuous rumble, as if a boat were idling roughly at a dock somewhere far off.

I was exhausted after our long trip, but too nervous to sleep easily. I thought I wouldn't try to sleep at all, but in a few minutes, without thinking, I was undressed and lying down on the broad bed, staring up at a dark ceiling where fluorescent decals of the moon and some stars reminded me of my childhood. Soon my eyes closed, my mind calmed, and I slept soundly.

The next day dawned bright, sun streaming through the blinds, my room so warm that I threw the covers off; my skin was damp from the humidity. I wanted to sleep longer, so I got up to close the blinds. From the window I saw two men and a woman with their backs to me, talking animatedly and gesturing toward the water, which I could now see was so vast that the land on the other side was only a puce-tinged smudge of chalk. I tried to see what they saw, but the lay of the land and the position of my room blocked my view. Curious, I decided to give up sleeping and got dressed, splashing myself at the sink rather than taking time for a shower. In a little while I was walking down the long hallway in search of the door I imagined would let me out onto the lawn; but not knowing my way, I ended up at the front of the house, where breakfast was being served in the huge dining room, and where the chatter of guests drowned out my curiosity.

Richard was sitting with some people at a large table near a window, the newspaper in heaps around him as he looked at the editorial page. "Good morning," he said. "You couldn't sleep either?" I told him about the people on the lawn, and he said I should have some melon, and we'd investigate. But of course as soon as breakfast was served I lost interest in anything but the food: fresh-cut fruit, hot muffins, rashers and poached eggs with cream sauce. I hadn't realized how hungry I was, having, as usual, not eaten much while traveling. Before I knew it, an hour had passed and Richard was folding his paper. By the time we found the door to the veranda and stood looking out over the lawn, whatever had attracted such attention had disappeared.

I know now what I then only sensed: that Richard had planned this odd holiday so far from home to cure our ailing marriage. In one way, it worked, for those first weeks persist in memory as the happiest we ever spent. Ironically, our taking separate rooms did the trick: being alone was refreshing, and sneaking through the halls late at night gave us back some of our earlier passion. We let people think we were a brother and sister traveling together; this explained both our separate rooms and our intimacy, and made it possible to flirt with others. So our "trysts" became loaded with the thrill of the forbidden, our kisses deeper because they were incestuous, stolen kisses. We took every chance we could to meet in secret, to sneak off alone, always pretending to be afraid of getting caught; in dark corners we fondled each other, hearts pounding, and then tried to return to the group composed and cool.

No one, not even Emmanuel or the concierge, knew that we were married, and so before long we were each "courted" by singles on the lookout for a summer fling. Richard made friends with a young woman from the coast—"laughing Lydia" he called her to me, because she giggled at everything he said. I was targeted by a man named Thomas who always wore a green jacket and tinted glasses. However friendly we were the rest of the time, however much we encouraged them, we only laughed at them later, in Richard's bed or mine, where we met late at night to eat the leftover sweets we'd hidden in our pockets at dinnertime, and to make love.

The days passed, and as we enjoyed ourselves, I almost forgot our arrival, and that first morning's minor mystery. Then one morning I woke up early again in the heat, and went to the window and looked out, and saw this time a small crowd of people, all facing the water, gesturing and talking. If they had been standing in an art gallery, they might have been discussing some bizarre new painting; one man turned to his companion, said something, laughed; she laughed and put her hand to his chest as if to push him away, and I imagined her saying, "Don't be ridiculous!"

I stood watching them for a moment, and then I got dressed, and this time went straight to the now-familiar door onto the big veranda, and stepped out. But just then the breakfast bell rang, and a slow-moving crowd pushed into me like a wave, sweeping me back toward the house and dining room. It didn't occur to me to stop someone and ask—I was determined to get through and see for myself, and when they had passed, I rushed down the steps to the lawn, looked out at the lake, and saw . . . nothing but the sun low and bright on the water. As I stood there perplexed, I heard the sound again:

the low rumble of an engine, a little louder this time, though softer and softer as I listened, and soon out of hearing. Disgusted, I turned to go inside and caught sight of Richard climbing the trellis up to the veranda; he had vaulted down and run to the cove in hope of seeing whatever it was, but the growth on either side was so thick that, short of jumping into the water fully clothed, he couldn't see around it. And the look on his face told me he had almost swum out, clothes or no; his curiosity was already greater than mine.

Now the sound became a distraction for us, a game, and an obsession, the sort of obsession that grows out of boredom and lack of imagination. We tried to get up as early as we could, to meet by the veranda doors, but the batteries in my travel clock failed, or we forgot to open the blinds so the sun would wake us, or we just slept through it all. In any case, it seemed we'd never get what we wanted. At lunch one day Richard said, "You know, I don't think we really want to know. It's more fun not knowing. There's no other explanation." In that case, I said, we should wait until the last day, and then stay awake the night before if we had to; we had to get up early for our train anyway. But this plan assumed that "it" came every morning, and we didn't want to take that chance.

Richard asked Lydia; I asked Thomas; neither of them had heard or seen a thing, but then neither of them got up before ten or eleven in the morning, since they usually stayed up nights playing cards and drinking. So my husband and I began to widen our circle of acquaintances quite deliberately, to find someone who had seen the mysterious, had heard the sound. Honeymooning couples, traveling sisters, mothers and children, old men and young—no one admitted it, or even seemed to know what we were talking about. I searched the dining room for the faces I had seen from my room, but the hotel was large and the clientele endlessly changing, and I had only seen two faces clearly, and those in profile. Day after day we got up as early as we could, even giving up sex to get to bed earlier so we could get up sooner, but we couldn't seem to fall asleep before midnight and we always woke up well past dawn. Emmanuel drove into town, a trip of some hours, and bought new batteries for my clock; I set it carefully before I went to sleep, but the next day found it fallen over so that the alarm button was pushed off, and of course by then it was too late.

One day in the last week of our visit it occurred to me to approach Emmanuel, who had been very helpful our whole stay. I asked him, first, quite cagily, Were there any boats that traveled the lake? I thought I might like to see the other shore. But he shook his head, apologizing. Aside from a few paddle boats for the pleasure of the guests, he knew of nothing, and the hotel was the only development on the lake as yet. Was there, then, I asked, a plane, perhaps with pontoons, that flew over the lake? "No," he said, "none that I know of." Finally, I said, had he seen guests go down to the beach some mornings to watch something? Mornings, he said, he had to help in the kitchen preparing breakfast, a process that began well before dawn. Did the kitchen windows face the lake? I asked. "No, ma'am," he said, the kitchen had no windows but was underground, and as hot as a sauna because of it. Finally I explained to him what I had seen and heard, but it was no good: he hadn't seen anything, or heard anything, or heard any of the guests talking about anything. A small part of me suspected him of lying, but I couldn't imagine why he would.

That day we were given box lunches, and a boy from the village came to lead us on a walk through the woods, to point out the varieties of trees and flowers. Only a few of the guests had signed up to go, but Richard and I had agreed that we'd meet with the group so we could talk about what I'd found out from Emmanuel. Five or six of the older ladies and Lydia and Thomas and Richard were waiting under an oak as I came up. Richard questioned me with his eyes; I shook my head slightly and raised an empty palm. Touching his beard, he seemed to disappear inside himself, and when the crowd of nature-lovers turned to begin their walk, he followed, so I did too.

At the hotel the day had seemed hot, but in the woods the air was cool and dry, the path clear though carpeted with lichen that crunched under our heels. I could hardly understand the guideboy, who was not more than fifteen years old and spoke in the dialect of his region. But he delighted in showing us everything, naming even the lichen we walked on ("British soldier" because of its red tip) and the fungi that grew on the dark trunks of some trees. We moved slowly, stopping often to hear a short dissertation on a leaf or insect; I don't think we traveled more than a mile before we entered a clearing on the lake, where we stopped for lunch. Richard and I found a spot for ourselves, not caring anymore about keeping up our charade; we nibbled at our sandwiches while Lydia and Thomas watched us with jealous eyes. I was tired, suddenly, of all of it—of the place, of the mystery, of the games. I felt that Richard was tired, too, sapped of energy. We needed each other, we needed the solace of ordinary intimacy more than we needed the contrived passion of the past month. There in the green of the woods we felt old and tired, and I wanted just to lay my head in his lap and sleep.

Just then the guideboy approached and squatted nearby, chewing a blade of grass; no one had fixed him a lunch. Richard offered him one of our sandwiches, which he took and swallowed in two bites; then he drank some of our water and ate a cupcake. Not a word was exchanged until he'd had his fill; then Richard, as if he'd had an idea, called the boy closer and whispered to him so that only I and the boy could hear: Did he know of a craft that passed by the hotel, early in the mornings, something with an engine, something we might like to see? The boy smiled immediately, his teeth dirty with chocolate, and nodded. Would he take us to see it? More nodding, and a time was set: that evening after dinner, he would meet us by the same oak.

The other guests, having finished their lunches, started to move around, and the boy jumped up and began talking loudly again about the last part of our walk, which would take us along the shore, where the willows . . . Richard and I followed, hardly paying attention, each of us imagining what the boy would show us that night. What could it be? Now I heard the sound, inside myself, that low growl turning, turning, turning. I couldn't tell what Richard was thinking; he seemed far away. I took his arm, but he didn't notice, and since he was walking faster than I wanted to, I finally let him go ahead, where he disappeared into the crowd of weary hikers lifting their feet carefully over tree roots exposed along the shore.

Back at the hotel, I couldn't find him, so I went to my room to bathe and dress; at dinner, I had to sit with Thomas and Lydia, who had finally discovered each other and sat smirking at Richard's absence.

But when the time came, he was there, at the tree. He hadn't taken time to bathe or change; his shoes were muddy, and bits of twigs hung from his beard. He seemed out of breath, and didn't speak except to hush me when he heard the boy coming. Catching sight of us, the boy stood at the edge of the woods and beckoned us to follow him along the same path as before. Richard must have offered him some prize or reward, I thought, and for some reason the thought made me angry.

As anxious as I'd been to know the secret, now I lagged behind. The boy had no lantern or light, but it was an easy path, and when I lost sight of them, I could still hear their voices and the crunch of their steps and followed that. In a few moments I entered the clearing where we'd eaten lunch; a small fire burned there, maybe as a signal. Nearby Richard and the boy sat, looking out at the lake, their faces lit like masks. Richard heard me and called me over; I sat next to him and felt his warm, absentminded arm comfortably around me. My heart beat in my throat. "He says it'll be here soon," Richard told me, whispering. I held his hand and looked toward the lake. "Soon," I heard the boy say, and then something else in dialect, to which Richard nodded and spoke a word I didn't recognize—a foreign word. Under the moon, the lake was a sheet of dark glass, and over the hiss of the fire I could hear the sound, faint but growing louder. It was a pitch-black night; back at the hotel, the cardplayers were already hard at it, while more conservative guests sat safe in their rooms or reading in the library; some, maybe, had stolen into the kitchen for a late-night snack. But here were my husband and I, and some strange boy, by a fire on the shore of the lake. We might as well have been in the middle of nowhere. The sound grew louder, and I thought I saw the water ripple, and then came a light. When the boy at last shouted, I put my face to Richard's shoulder and started to cry.

It was only a garbage scow, in the tow of a tugboat lit by kerosene lanterns, that came each morning early to take away

the trash of the guests, to dump it on another shore. Its driver
was the boy's father, a lunatic who for our benefit wore a tourist's discarded dress and danced a jig, his white and hairy legs
bare beneath the skirt. It was only a garbage scow, so filthy
that we could smell it from shore.

The season drew to a close. Slowly the crowd dwindled until
few of us remained. The larger part of the dining room was
shut off by Oriental screens, and many of the staff left for their
homes in the city. A hush descended over the hotel. Richard
and I at last unpacked the books we'd brought to read, and sat
quiet for hours—on the veranda, in the library, alone in our
separate rooms—our heads bent, like a priest and a nun at
penance.

The morning we were to leave, I got up before dawn to
bathe and pack the remainder of my things. It was then, as I
stood in front of the vanity filling my small bag, that I glanced
out the window and saw, again, a man and a woman staring
off toward the lake. With nothing left to do, I decided to join
them. But the water was calm, the air silent as I came up beside
them—no sign of the mad garbage man and his smelly craft. I
asked the woman where it was, but she only looked at me
uncomprehending and, when I explained myself, shook her
head, gesturing toward the far shore. At first I saw nothing at
all; then I saw that there was nothing to see. Just the rising
sun, the reddened sky, and the lake below it, glowing like an
ember.

The Chef's Bride

The chef was a Greek named George who dragged his words through English thickly, like a wagon through mud. For years he had lived alone in the one-room apartment provided for him at the back of the restaurant, and scarcely anyone ever saw him on the street or in the shops, or out of his tall white cap, double-breasted white coat, and blue-and-white checked pants. (Not that they would have recognized him if they had.) He was large but not yet obese, with a glossy red face and little hair, and under his hat he kept a damp handkerchief with which he mopped the sweat from his brow. The waitresses thought him a kind man—mostly because, despite the owner's warnings, he gave them things to eat: bits of steak, fried potatoes, the smallest shrimp. Besides, he had a jovial face and laughed easily at whatever they said.

The sous-chef was a younger man who had worked a year as dishwasher before being promoted, on the occasion of the former sous-chef's quitting. He too was large but not obese, and wore a double-breasted coat, but he had no hat and wore stained brown trousers rather than the traditional checked pants. It was his job to cut and slice, to dice and measure, to hand the necessary ingredients to the chef as he cooked—and on Monday mornings and when the chef was ill, to take over the cooking himself. After several years he was still clumsy at his work and sometimes ruined three eggs before one was poached correctly; he was a dark man with a low brow and a surly temperament, as if he blamed his ineptitude on the world. He walked eyes down, neck thrust forward like a horse's, and Horse was what the waitresses called him.

There was a rumor of something between the sous-chef and

the dishwasher, a woman older than he with yellow hair and two teeth whose absence made her speak with a lisp. There was little enough reason for the rumor; no one had ever seen them together except during their breaks, when they stood in the courtyard, smoking cigarettes and exchanging low words punctuated by the woman's cackling laugh. But the waitresses were a close-knit band of marriageable girls, so the slightest hint of romance titillated them, and the idea of an affair between the sous-chef and the dishwasher all the more so, since it seemed so utterly unlikely. Sometimes the waitresses pretended to flirt with him, to see if the dishwasher would notice, but she was stolid in her steamy realm, imperturbable in her rubber apron.

One summer the chef got married. No one knew about it until afterward, and no one knew anything about his bride except what he told them: that she was Greek and beautiful and had agreed to marry him sight unseen—he made much of that. No one knew that he had chosen her when she was still a child playing on the cobblestone street of the little village of his birth, or that when he decided to marry he wrote her parents extolling his own virtues and sent them money hidden between the pages of a soiled menu. She came to the chef by plane from Athens, and had gone to Athens with her father on the big ferryboat; it was the first time she had ever been away from the island where she was born. She arrived laden with clothing and dowry: gold necklaces around her neck, heavy lace tablecloths pinned under her black skirt like coarse slips. By taxi the chef took her from the airport to the justice of the peace, and from there back to the restaurant, where he whisked her inside wordlessly and back through the kitchen door to his little apartment. There he unwrapped her as if she were a piece of bone china. She was fourteen and knew only to do as she was told.

Despite the chef's boasts to his bride's parents, the restaurant was in fact small and undistinguished, with red-flocked wallpaper, a mustard gold carpet, simple meals, and a noisy, smoke-filled lounge through which the diners had to pass to arrive at the dining room. Yet one evening late that summer, the place was transformed. A huge wedding party, hundreds of guests elegant in tuxedos and gowns, flooded the rooms where new white linens and roses glowed in candlelight; the silver shone, the crystal sang. The chef prepared an elaborate meal, a meal so perfect that the bride and groom, themselves transplanted Greeks, came into the kitchen to congratulate him. They brought champagne—the cheap stuff, of course, but champagne nonetheless. The bride's gown swept the dirty floor as she glided toward him with the scent of flowers and a kiss waiting on her lips. Then, while the wedding guests drank and danced in the ballroom, the chef poured champagne for the waitresses, and they had their own party in the dingy kitchen, telling stories, getting drunk. One of the girls sat on his lap, tickling her cheek on his stubbly beard as he fed her crumbs of wedding cake. Meanwhile, back in the dish room, the sous-chef and the dishwasher drank from their own bottles, lounging against the stainless steel counter.

In the little apartment, the chef's bride sat, as she liked to, by the open window, looking out into the courtyard, where a few young gingko trees slept, heavy with leaf, deeply shadowed. Between the restaurant's twin chimneys in a chink of sky, stars glittered like bits of broken mirror. The door to the restaurant kitchen stood propped open to the courtyard, letting cooler air inside and the sounds of celebration out. Behind and around her in the unlit room, heat radiated from the furniture as it would from concrete, from brick, from cobblestone. There were a sofa bed, a table and chairs, a small, nearly empty refrigerator, two bureaus, and a shelf of books and magazines. This, and the view from the window, had been the first month of her married life. She hadn't dared venture out; she spoke only Greek and was shy as well as young and unschooled. Besides, the chef worked long days, from before dawn and sometimes, like tonight, until after midnight, and had off only Monday mornings, when the sous-chef cooked breakfast. The chef had no time for sight-seeing, no time for a honeymoon. So he had patiently explained.

But it didn't matter. The girl was content with the novelty of marriage, content to sit by the window and watch and wait for him. At odd times, when business was slow inside, he brought her meals to her, and kissed her then, and left the covered dishes. At night when he finally came home they pulled the mattress out, and she lay down on it, motionless and silent while he washed himself at the sink, hoping that when he came to bed he would pull her over to straddle his belly, to ride him like a pony. He often did. The novelty of this, too, she enjoyed, although at first it had been difficult.

That night in the heat she wore only a loose underslip of white cotton so sheer that it took on the color of her skin. She could see the brown coronas of her nipples, large and flat, and the curve of breast around them. She was pregnant; she didn't know it yet, but would soon.

She remembered the morning when her mother had sat with her on the narrow cot in her room and told her about the chef. Sunlight fell in a clear square from the window onto the floor, and as her mother talked, the girl looked at her feet caught in that slow-moving square of light, her brown feet browner against the whitewashed floor. Her mother's voice rose and fell and quavered. The air was warm, but cool too; dry and filled with a clean, papery scent. She turned one foot, looked at her long toes, the curve of her arch, and wondered what it meant to fly, to be in a foreign country, to marry a man you had never seen. She surprised herself: she was not afraid. She thought it must be that she was brave and trusted the judgment of her parents. Now her mother was crying, but what did that mean? Only that her mother would miss her, miss her helping with the younger children, miss her baking the fat Os of bread, miss her taking the bread down to the wharf for her father to tear a chunk from, to eat while he worked.

She remembered her father taking her to the mainland, and she remembered Piraeus, the port city where people swarmed like bees, ducking in and out of doors, hovering over merchandise strewn on the sidewalks, bumping into one another without a word of apology or even recognition. Half-naked sun-burnished women strode about, their bare arms linked with those of men. She followed her father, who seemed to know his way, until they found the bus to Athens.

In Athens the buildings were tall, and the people dressed in bright colors and seemed unable to keep their eyes focused on their destinations. Her father led her up a steep hill to the apartment building of her uncle, his brother. The family celebrated that night, drinking brandy in toast to her prestigious marriage. Later, with her young cousins, she watched television for the first time, a western, and saw film of the land where she was going to be married. It was flat, dry, dusty—not so very different from home, she thought.

When her father left her at the plane the next day, like her mother he cried; she embraced him and went aboard with the strange, sudden sensation of having passed into the next life.

She dozed at the apartment window, and dreamed. In her dream, the chef became a sheep and she disemboweled him, planning a roast to feed her family. Her mother was there, and her father, and her younger brothers and sisters, who stuck their fingers in the bucket of entrails and drew them out to suck off the salty blood. The chef looked at her with his red, sweat-beaded face and said, in Greek, "You must tear off the fell, then plant garlic in the fat underneath, here and there, like seeds."

She woke with a shiver. There were voices in the courtyard: a man, a woman; a white coat, bleached hair. It was the sous-chef and the dishwasher. She recognized the woman's laugh, high-pitched with desperation, and the man's dark pants. Every morning she had seen them, sharing cigarettes with a peculiar camaraderie, like children pretending to be adults. Usually they stood just outside the kitchen door, but tonight they were against the far wall, where no doubt they believed themselves in shadow, not realizing the strength of the moon. The girl watched the sous-chef run his hands along the woman's body, watched his back as he struggled with the buttons of her blouse, keeping his face buried in her neck. Now and then the dishwasher struck him, in the back or shoulder, but gently—not as if she meant to hurt him. Then she stopped and seemed suddenly to embrace him, suspended between his heavy body and the brick wall, her hands clasping his fleshy shoulders, her skirt hiked and bare legs around his waist. Slowly he began to push himself against her, like one dog against another, his buttocks greenish in the moonlight. In her window, the girl shivered and remembered a night when she had come in upon her own parents making love in their moonlit bed, haunch to haunch like two goats in the field.

Afterward, the sous-chef dressed himself, said a few low words, and went back into the kitchen. The dishwasher seemed less hurried. Her blouse still unbuttoned, her skirt askew, she gazed up at something in the sky so that her face was lit by the moon. For the first time the girl saw that under the mask of age was a child's face, young and deeply sad. She drew back into the shadows, suddenly afraid to be seen; when she looked again, the dishwasher was gone.

That night when the chef returned, full of champagne and dreams of endless weddings, endless success, he fell onto the bed and began instantly to sleep the noisy, leaden sleep of the drunk. The girl watched him for a while, then, matching her breaths to his, fell asleep herself.

Where had the dishwasher gone? For two days the waitresses wondered and covered for her, worried but sure she'd reappear any moment. Then the mystery was solved: a fisherman found her body, caught on the rocks in the river shallows. She had drowned, the coroner declared; yet he suspected foul play: her shoulders and buttocks were bruised, as if she'd fallen backward. But a motive could not be found, for the woman had no association in town save the sous-chef, who denied knowing a thing.

Not wanting to frighten her, the chef told his bride nothing about the incident but simply gave her the dish room, thinking to keep her close to him, safe from the world outside. And neither did she tell him what she had seen, but simply took the job and slowly began to fit into her new world, to learn the language, to understand.

Within the year she gave birth to a healthy boy. Sometimes, as she fed him, she sat again by her window and watched the sous-chef take his morning breaks, glowering and unhappy as ever, smoking his yellow cigarettes alone in the dusty courtyard.

Sleepwalker

At first, I smelled the cigarette smoke only on weekends. Neither Karen nor I smoked; I never had, and Karen had stopped when we got married. For a while I wondered if she could be smoking behind my back, but try as I might I couldn't find a trace of evidence anywhere: no ashes in the bathroom waste basket, nothing on her breath, no burnt matches stuck behind things. Besides, if she wanted to smoke again, she would've had the nerve to do it in front of me. Yet there was the smell of smoke, every Saturday, every Sunday, especially in the morning. It spoiled the weekend for me.

When this had gone on for several weeks, I waited till Saturday to make sure it would happen again, and then I pointed it out to Karen. "Do you smell that?" I said. "It smells like . . ."

"It's de Ford, Peter."

"What?"

"He's home on weekends."

Our neighbor in the duplex was a traveling salesman we rarely saw. On his mailbox and next to his doorbell he'd stuck little labels, the kind you make with a gun that presses the letters into plastic strips; these read, simply, D. Ford. So Karen and I called him "de Ford." Friends coming over thought we meant that he drove a Ford, but he didn't, he drove a Toyota, which was always full—I remembered now—of cigarette samples and display placards.

"So he doesn't just sell them?" I said.

"Maybe he moonlights as a taste tester."

That solved who, but still something bothered me. "How's the smoke getting in?" I said, and went into the bedroom closet, which ran the length of the only shared wall between our places, a set of mirror-twin condo flats that, from above, must have looked like a flattened barbell with squared ends. Inside the closet I sniffed. The smell was stronger, of course, but diffuse; I couldn't tell where it was coming from. I got down on my hands and knees and crawled along the floor of the closet, pushing shoes out of my way. I heard Karen come in.

"Peter," she said. "You're going to put everything back just the way you found it."

"I'm looking for the gap," I said.

"What?"

"The gap in the wall. Those cheap bastards, they must not have bothered to finish the closet. Figured we wouldn't see it."

"So complain to the manager," Karen said.

"I will—don't worry."

"What?"

She couldn't hear me; I had my face down to the floor.

"Eureka!" I said. In the far corner of the closet was a hole big enough for me to stick my finger through. I heard a scraping sound on the other side.

"Who's in there?" said D. Ford.

That should have been the end of it, but then strange things started to happen. First, one morning Karen went to the door to leave for school—I was working at home, in my studio—and found the door unlocked. "Honey," she called.

"Yeah?"

"Have you been out this morning?"

"No."

"Well, why's the door unlocked?"

You see, because of the burglar alarm, we had an elaborate system of checks and balances before going to bed, and there was no way that door could be unlocked unless someone had turned off the alarm and unlocked it after we'd done our routine. The couple of times we had turned the alarm on without locking the doors and windows, we'd woken up half the neighborhood. The alarm sounded like a cross between a siren and a banshee wail, with a little bit of elephant trumpeting thrown in for good measure, but it took us a minute, the first couple of times, to figure out what the noise was, and by then lights were coming on up and down the block. It was a neighborhood of condos, all more or less alike, although we'd been assured that every unit was unique; ours, for instance, joined with de Ford's at the "spacious bedroom" (more specifically at the "dual walk-in closet"), then opened up from there into the "beautiful living area" (combo living room/dining room/ kitchen) with "cathedral ceiling," which gave off onto the "breakfast nook," which was the glassed-in porch I used as my studio, and an "entertainment room," where Karen had her study. Anyway, people who'd bought into this deal clearly had not done so in order to be disturbed at midnight, which was when Karen and I generally got to bed.

So if the door was unlocked, someone must have turned the alarm off and opened it—from the inside. "Ghosts?" I said.

"In a year-old condo?"

"Remember *Poltergeist?*"

Karen put her briefcase down and stood looking at me. She was very pretty in the morning, with her fresh hair and makeup. But then she was very pretty even just out of the shower, dripping wet.

"We are not standing on an unpurged cemetery, are we?" I shrugged my shoulders. "I guess we forgot to turn the alarm on," she said, and picked her stuff up again. "Meet me for lunch?"

"All right," I said. But I felt something uneasy in my chest, which at the time I thought was healthy fear. We'll have to be more careful, I thought, from now on.

After this, a bunch of little things. First, a book I had been reading the night before was tampered with. I knew I had only got through page 113; when I picked the book up the next evening, it was open to page 187. I asked Karen if she'd touched it; she hadn't. I asked her if we had a maid I didn't know about; she said not unless I had hired her, and if I had, she wanted to know about it. We gave each other a puzzled smirk. Another mystery. I turned back to page 113 and began to read; what I read seemed familiar to me, and since I knew I hadn't read it before, I decided the book was derivative and put it down.

Then in general we began to notice, mornings, that things around the house weren't as they usually were. A bag of potato chips had been raided, emptied, and left in the cupboard—not anything we would do. Both of us were very conscious about keeping things clean around the house so we wouldn't get bugs. I had this theory that a new building like ours would never see a roach if we handled our garbage the right way: I'd bought an expensive garbage can with a lid that bolted on, and a smaller one like it for the bathroom, although what a roach would want in there I didn't know. That was another thing we found one morning: the lid of the garbage can off, sitting to one side of it. And then we found tumblers half full of juice on the coffee table, a magazine open to an article about skin moisturizers, and the television set left on—soundless, but scary anyway, like finding a stranger busy in the corner of your living room when you expected to be alone.

If it wasn't ghosts, then it had to be either Karen or me. We both knew this, but for a while we didn't talk about it. I guess we thought we were each protecting the other's right to privacy. Naturally, I was sure it was Karen; she had a history of insomnia, but maybe she was afraid to tell me that she wasn't sleeping well, for fear I'd worry, or maybe she was walking in her sleep and didn't know it. Karen confessed later to thinking I had a lover, and was waking up to go whisper on the phone to her. But she couldn't figure out why I'd be so sloppy about it, leaving all those clues. Each of us secretly tried to stay awake at night, to catch the other at it, but that didn't work. Actually, we were both sleeping soundly.

Finally one morning Karen found her car facing opposite the direction she'd left it in the night before; someone had moved it and then backed it into her space, which she never did. She confessed to me that one other time, about a week before, she'd come out to find her car moved, and the driver's seat flipped forward, as if somebody'd used the back seat too.

"Why didn't you tell me?" I said. "How could you keep something like that from me?"

She got defensive, but what did I expect? "Listen," she said. She had that look, the one with the square jaw and narrow eyes. "I don't know what's going on any more than you do. And I don't know, anymore, if I can trust you. Understand?"

I understood. I felt the same way about her. We looked at each other guiltily, confessed what had been going through our heads, laughed over it awhile, and then hatched a scheme.

Whichever one of us it was—because by then it was obvious that one of us was sleepwalking (I knew it wasn't me)—had got in the habit of reading on the living-room couch. That explained my book, the magazine, and the newspaper being disorganized a couple of times. Now, the carpet in our living room, stuff we chose and had installed ourselves, was a thick, bone white wool pile. Beautiful, but with one drawback: it picked up and held footprints. We'd agonized over this the first few weeks but in the end had grown used to it. Now it seemed the perfect way to trap our sleepwalker.

So one night before we went to bed, we added something to our routine: grooming the carpet. It was a two-step procedure. First we ran the vacuum to fluff up the pile; then we took a one-by-four left over from bookshelf building and, starting in the middle, sort of scraped it over the surface of the carpet, backing up to the edge, until the area all around the sofa was like a fresh blanket of snow, ready for prey.

But our sleepwalker was wily. Several nights running, it was no show. We'd get up in the morning and run in to see . . . nothing. Virgin carpet. "Well," Karen said. "Maybe we've cured ourselves." She was careful to talk in the plural, but I knew she thought it was me. In the back of my mind, I thought she might be right, but I wasn't willing to admit anything yet. "Maybe," I said, suspiciously.

At the time, I was working to get a new client. A new bank was opening a branch in town, and they wanted a campaign to launch it. One of the ad agencies I free-lanced for had decided I was their man; they'd given me a month to come up with something, a theme, the works: billboards, radio and television spots, newspaper ads, promotional gimmicks. After two weeks, I still had virtually nothing. I felt like Darren Stevens on "Bewitched," only Karen couldn't bail me out the way Samantha could him. I'd sit and stare at the information they'd sent me about the bank, historical stuff mostly, but I couldn't get a handle on it. It bored me.

I knew from experience that the only way to get interested in something like that was to get interested in it. I'd given Karen that advice plenty of times when she had a paper to write, which was something she hated about grad school. (She'd gone back to study her first love, theater; I was putting her through.) But it's the only thing I know about creativity: getting started is easy once you get started. Yet day after day I sat there staring and got nowhere. That's when I started again to smell—or thought I did—the cigarette smoke, at odd times of day, when the air moved a certain way. But when I looked outside, de Ford's Toyota was gone. It was spooky.

I hadn't told Karen any of this. I had a lot of pride when it came to my work, and when I'd gone free-lance a year after we were married, I'd made much ado of my confidence, and she'd bought my story—hook, line, and sinker. Although so far it'd been going well enough to keep us in cash, a lot rested on this particular job, the bank job. I could prove myself to Karen and to the rest of the ad agencies around town if I could just get this campaign. To begin, to begin.

So I had plenty of reasons not to sleep well, but I did. I slept like a baby.

We still did our number with the carpet; even though we were starting to lose interest and the problem seemed resolved, Karen kept saying, "One more night." And it paid off. Finally, one morning, Karen got up before me to put some coffee on.

"Honey," she called. "Come here."

I was groggy with sleep and had really thought I might stay in bed another hour, but I understood the tone of her voice and got myself up.

On the coffee table the newspaper was spread out like a placemat for the crumby plate and half-drunk glass of milk that sat in the middle of it. And an ashtray, containing two cigarette butts. (Later on we found a pile of them, dumped in the shrubs out back.) And, walking up to the couch, in front of the couch, walking away from the couch: footprints. Big, barefoot footprints. Size eleven. My footprints.

"I think you should see someone," Karen said, for about the fiftieth time.

I kept quiet.

"Why not?"

It was hard for me to speak. "Remember when we first met? When you had that problem? And you couldn't sleep?"

"This is different," Karen said, with a warning flag on the end of *different*.

"We worked it out," I said.

"This isn't the same."

What was so different? I wanted to know. "Peter," she said, bringing her weather-girl hands together as if she were about to pray. "The difference is this: I *knew* what was wrong, I *knew* I wasn't sleeping, and I knew why, too. Guilt, pure and simple. But you . . ." She paused and pointed at me, as if I were a storm front in eastern Iowa. "You didn't even know *what* you were doing. And you *still* don't know why." She gave me a long, slow look and shook her head. "You don't get it, do you?"

"No," I said. "It'll probably stop now—I mean, now that I know . . ."

"I've known it was you for a while," she said. I looked at her. "No, not the whole time. Not quite. But I don't sleep that well when I'm worried, and you're no butterfly on your feet. One night I heard you get up, and I followed you. Do you know what you did?"

"What?"

She told me then. How I had gotten up and pulled on an old T-shirt. How I had walked around the apartment as if I were looking for something. How I had finally gone out the back door, naked from the waist down, and peed into one of her potted roses. How I had come back inside then, and cooked myself an egg, and even washed the frying pan. Stuff I would never, never do.

She hadn't dared to wake me up, she said, because she'd

heard it was dangerous, psychologically. "But the second time you took my car out . . . I followed you, and you just drove around, but I almost went crazy, I was so scared you'd get in a wreck. That's when I decided to do something. You know you'd never have believed it unless there was proof." We both looked down at the rug, at my footprints in it.

"Trapped," I said, "like a bug in a rug." Karen didn't laugh. She just kept looking at me, waiting.

"Look," I said. I took a deep breath; it hurt because I was feeling a lot of pain in my chest, like something was boxed in there—a feeling I'd had for a long time without really knowing it. "I guess we'd better talk."

We talked a long time. Months. To each other, and to some other folks too. If I could make a drawing of what we said, it would be a landscape. Close up would be particular plants, rendered realistically, grass plants with tiny, almost invisible flowers; a wild rose, like the ones Karen was growing on the patio; and some other growing things, unidentifiable but somehow familiar. Weeds, some vegetables maybe. Farther back things would stretch into miles of undifferentiated green, with a few trees here and there, the big, lonely kind stuck in the middle of fields, the kind I've never understood why farmers leave standing. Somewhere there'd be water, like a blue snake weaving through the pasture.

But beyond this would be a city, seen vaguely through the mist, a dark, large, ominous, and seductive city silhouetted against a sky so blue that the buildings and the white clouds, the whole landscape, would seem superimposed on it—the way sky looks in postcards, an unbelievable sky, a professional sky. But I've seen it in real life, on certain days. In comparison to this kind of sky, everything seems small.

In the end I gave up that bank job, and jobs like it; I just realized it wasn't my cup of tea. Karen took a teaching assistantship to cover her tuition, and we sold the condo and bought a run-down old house to fix up. It's in a kind of seedy part of town, but it's the prettiest house I've ever seen, with gingerbread, a wraparound porch, and windows seven feet high, and a yard around it where Karen's planning a garden.

I can't really explain why we moved, or how this was part of the solution to our problems; it really doesn't save us any money. In fact, long before we even thought of moving, the biggest problem seemed to resolve itself, like a knot finally coming untied, leaving only the detail work to do. I can't really tell you how we did it; I can only tell you what we did. One morning, we got up and got started.

And we're still going.

Addison

Living next door to a funeral home has given me a chance, over the years, to observe the vagaries of death and mourning. From behind the dark screen of my porch, I've watched the departure of the hearse, sometimes only on its way to the car wash (it comes back wet and gleaming but empty) but sometimes returning an hour or so later with a body. Try as I may, I can't predict which. Both events are treated with equal dignity, which is to say that the mortician—funeral director, he calls himself—is as likely to wear a sport shirt as a suit, the radio blaringly tuned to a local station. If I happen to be at the back of the house when the hearse returns from a call, I can watch them unload the stretcher, the anonymous body under a white sheet or, more recently, zipped into a gray bag, cylindrical except for the small pyramid of the feet, and sometimes not even that: the feet of people who've been bedridden a long time curl under, like those of the Wicked Witch when Dorothy's house fell on her.

By now, the whole thing seems to me quite ordinary, quite simple—the delivery of a package, the performance of a service. At least, that is, until the family arrives to select a coffin. What I've noticed over the years is how death plays two tunes on mourners: their faces are contorted, shattered, frantic, uncontrolled, but at least alive, in motion, while from the neck down the posture is stiff, deadened, unnatural. Women who suffer as grieving women do—which is to say all women— should be able to throw themselves on the pavement of the driveway, to use their whole bodies to express their agony; men whose faces bear such awkward, angry expressions of discomfort should be allowed to strike out, to bash their fists against the brick wall of the funeral home until they bleed. It's impossible not to empathize with them, as they walk from their cars and up the steps; when the dead person is young, the crying is continuous and audible even inside my house, if the windows are open. Of an old person who dies, you can say, He had a good life. Of a young person, only, He might have had.

I've experienced my share of funerals, I think. My parents both died years ago; they'd divorced when I was young, and so I flew, in one case to Texas, in the other to New Jersey, and stood in the lines of mourners and received solace from relatives and friends, most of whom were strangers to me; and on both occasions, I cried, appropriately saddened. My mother was an alcoholic who had lived into her late sixties. In a sense, her death had been overdue; I cried not for the dead woman but for the woman I remembered caring for me as a child. On the other hand, I was quite broken up over the death of my father, who lived to be much older, and whom I had hardly known; perhaps all sons feel this way. Looking back, I think perhaps I felt guilty that I hadn't spent more time with him, hadn't tried harder to visit him. His funeral was better attended than my mother's, which made me think that perhaps he had been a good man, well liked, someone I might have enjoyed knowing. I remember the odd feeling of being in dry, hot, flat Texas, a state I'd never seen before, looking down at my father in his dark business suit, and wondering at the resemblance between us: the same face, really, at a different stage—my jaw, my mouth, my nose. Then I felt a rush of pain, and tears on my cheeks, and someone—a man who had known my father—put his arm around my shoulders without speaking, until I regained myself. I said, "It's all right," thanked him, and took my seat with the others to listen to the eulogy.

So I've grieved before, and watched others grieve, watched it all, from the body arriving, small and real, to the body leaving, enlarged by memory; I know the ritual by heart, the dignity and the indignity of it. And so, when Claire died, I should have been well prepared.

But the announcement came as a surprise. I'd seen her only a day or two before, and she'd seemed fine, much alive. We think of death, I suppose, as something that announces its presence clearly before it takes effect; and we think of life as something that hangs on, fights death. When I say we, of course, I mean I. This is how I have thought of death, of life; I see now I was mistaken.

I'd seen her on Tuesday, I think; on Friday I read the announcement in the newspaper, and although it was her name, and her age, and the details seemed correct, I was not convinced that it was Claire who had died until I went to the diner where she waitressed and saw for myself that she wasn't there.

I've eaten nearly half my meals at that diner since moving here over twenty years ago—then a young, new professor, full of preconceptions, picturing myself in a leather chair in a book-lined study, ancient trees shading my yard (this described our chairman's house, where I'd been feted during my interview). Disillusionment was swift, but somehow I got through it, and found this house, where the rent was cheap because of the location: most people are uneasy about mortuaries. Twenty years later I own the house, and in that book-lined room sits the leather chair and the grand piano I always wanted. But then I was a different man, young and naïve.

That man—the man I was—got off a bus one steamy August afternoon with a head full of figures, formulas, and proofs, theories and logic. He was a mathematician, just finished with school, and setting out to be a professor in the mathematics department of a small-town university. He arrived in that heat wearing a dark blue suit, as if he expected to be met at the station; of course, he was not. A cab took him to the motel where his reservations were; once in his room he quickly turned on the air-conditioner, which wheezed and growled and spewed forth something damp but not quite cool; he used the toilet and found the butt of a cigarette floating in it; he lay down on top of the thin, cobwebby sheets. But it was cheap.

He called the department and was informed that the chairman, like most of the faculty, was out of town for the summer break. And so he found himself alone, in a strange town, in a region he knew nothing about. He spent the afternoon feeling sorry for himself. There's no point in denying it: he was inexperienced enough to think that someone would have thought of him, thought to take care of his needs or at least offer help. He stared at the dusty ceiling of his room through the dimness, and nearly cried, as much from the unrelenting heat as from frustration. But as the day wore on into evening he came out of it; hunger does that for you, reminds you that you're on your own, that you have a body to feed.

The boy at the desk sent him to a diner down the road. He felt more than saw the pines towering alongside him as he walked, the insects buzzing, humming, clicking. Cars seemed to slow as they neared, then roared by; he knew he must look odd, in his wrinkled blue suit, in that heat, walking. He'd never learned to drive, having been born and raised in a city where it wasn't necessary, and having gone to school in another where the same was true. He'd have to learn now, he saw that; it was simply too hot to walk from place to place.

He found the diner, a flat-roofed building with slanting, mirrored windows that reflected the pickup trucks parked in front. Inside, a wall of cold air met him head on, and he stumbled, like a man come in from days on the desert, and found a table.

Someone handed him a menu; he took it blindly, and stared at it as if it were written in another language. A glass of something to drink appeared; at first he sipped, and then gulped; the glass was refilled with more strong, sweet, cold tea, and he raised his eyes.

"You look hot," said the waitress.

That was Claire. She was a blunt woman, not attractive but not unattractive: short and square, like a gas pump, with dark hair pulled back from a lined face and a mouth that seemed, at times, no friendlier than the edge of a razor blade, and that, when it smiled, smiled only thinly. Her name did not suit her; it was prettier than she was.

There was nothing innately special about her, nothing that made him, the young man, fall in love; so he did not fall in love. She was to him, and would always be, the fixture she seemed to be, working lunches and dinners six days a week, then going home to her apartment; she had been married once, had two boys, both teenage by the time he met her; she'd been divorced for years. She had a cat named Tully and kept two finches in a cage, mainly to entertain the cat while she was gone, and she drove a squat car with rusted hubcaps. On her night off she bowled with the league. And apart from this her life was unknown, unknowable; in fact, there seemed to be nothing more, and the young man Addison often pitied her.

Yet he returned to the diner every night that first week, until he found his house by the funeral home, and then he came—less regularly, but still came—for lunch or for dinner five or six or seven times a week. When friends from other parts of the country came to visit him, he took them to the diner; at their surprise (or dismay), he simply said, "They know me here, they'll take care of us. Besides, the food's authentic." And of course he could address Claire by name, and impress his friends that he had come to fit so well into the niche he had found for himself, although it did seem odd that a mathematics professor should eat most of his meals in this kind of red-neck bar and grill, where most of the other customers wore cowboy hats and boots, drank much, and ate little.

But hasn't everyone experienced something like this? Uneasy in a strange city, once we find places that comfort us, we tend to return to them. It feels good to have the cashier recognize us and accept a check without the usual ID, to have the gas station attendant ask about our trip to Chicago, to have a bartender say, "The usual?" and know what that means, to have a waiter say, "I think you'll like this," and know what he's talking about. The need to narrow our horizons, to make the world small enough to handle, to make it familiar, is a natural one, although perhaps Addison needed this more than most.

But something else happened to bind him to Claire. His second semester teaching, he became involved with a girl, a senior in his introductory class who had been doing so poorly that she began to come in for tutoring. She needed the course to complete her core, to graduate. It happened the way it always happens: the office, door closed for quiet and not for privacy, grows smaller with each appointment; leaning near to correct an error, he smells her perfume; one day they touch accidentally; the next, not so accidentally. The subject wandered; they held hands; they kissed. He was swept away.

Addison knew, of course, that it was wrong, but he couldn't think clearly in that heat, he couldn't think of the future at all; it was blacked out to him, like the eyes of people in photographs, people who do not want to be identified: he thought he recognized the mouth of it, but could not name the face. And things really didn't seem so bad, so dangerous.

The one thing you can always count on in academia is that the semester will end and a new one will begin. The girl came to him in tears; he thought, My god, she's pregnant, but no, she simply wanted to know what would happen after she graduated. Their affair till then had been carried on in secret, and she'd been happy enough with it: meeting twice a week, in his office, making hasty love on the pile of blankets he'd smuggled in, then sitting and talking in the afternoon light. Now she had the offer of a job in another town. Then she laid her last card down, and it was Love. Or so she said.

Addison arrived at the diner late that night. The bar was crowded with men watching some sport on television, and he had to speak loudly to be heard. He couldn't eat the food Claire brought him, and at last ordered a beer and had her take the plate away. The tables cleared, she took off her apron and hung it up, and came and sat down across from him.

"What is it?" she said.

Fumbling at first, he soon poured the story out. He told her everything. He was completely honest.

"Why don't you marry her?" she said. "It's what you want, or you wouldn't be debating. Besides, a man your age needs a wife."

In a flash Addison saw himself married to the girl— endlessly, endlessly. They had nothing in common, and they would argue or, worse, fall into perpetual silence; she was too young and would probably, eventually, cheat on him; she had majored in interior design and would want to redecorate his house her way, not his. He didn't know her at all, he suddenly realized. Their talk had been limited, to say the least; perhaps there wasn't really any her to know, yet. In his mind she now seemed only a warm, fleshy figure he had played with, enjoyed; beyond that, everything was vague, distorted, and— like all things unknown—fearful. Only one thing was certain: marriage to her would mean disaster, and was better avoided.

He looked at Claire. She gave him one of her grim smiles, and suddenly he saw how wise she was: with a few words she had swept away his doubt. She had made him face the truth by making him face his fears. He couldn't marry that girl; she was nothing to him. He saw their whole affair as a trap he was about to sidestep. "Thank you," he said, getting up, already rehearsing in his head what he would say to the girl, and when.

But had Claire meant that? I think not. For all I know, as he—as I—walked away, she sat there not realizing what conclusion I'd come to or why. I think now that I should have married the girl: she was lovely, and bright, and caring, and we got along well enough; I might even have been in love with her, just too stupid to know that fear can blind you. At least I should have given it more of a chance. Instead, though, the next day I called her; we met in my office, and I said how lovely it had been, and how, like all lovely things, it was too perfect to last. And then I told her that she'd be getting an A in my course. I'm surprised she didn't slap me and bring charges; it speaks well of her that she did not.

After this, the young man Addison, my former self, had other flings, affairs—never again with a student but with a young, redheaded visiting instructor who finally left for a tenure-track position at a better school, and with a friend of a friend, a divorcée with three children. Of course, she'd wanted marriage and was angry when it didn't come to that, but he had never "deceived" her: their assumptions had simply been different from the start. In the years that followed, he'd dated a few women, but becoming "involved" with them had seemed . . . only something you did if you wanted sex, and eventually sex lost its charm. It had only been a novelty in any case, never an obsession.

Instead, the years filled themselves with other things. He strove to become a virtuoso at the piano, and late into the night would play Tchaikovsky with wild abandonment, assured that nothing could disturb his neighbors, the dead. Toward owning a grand piano he bought and restored lesser instruments, reselling them at good profit; he learned not only to refinish the wood but to restore the sound, which was his proudest accomplishment. When the grand was brought into the house, he felt as full of life and love as if he had just observed the birth of his child. The analogy is not bad: doors off their hinges, the piano was squeezed, barely, through the openings and into the house, then was placed, adjusted, settled in front of the bay window that looked out onto the side yard and its tangle of shrubs and vines and the funeral home beyond.

He took lessons, too, from the master at the university, and gave recitals, and became part of a crowd to whom music was the balm that allowed them to continue life in what they called "this godforsaken town."

But he had never, after that first day, truly felt forsaken. He had his house, his work, his pianos, his cashier at the grocery store, his attendant at the gas station. He had the diner, and Claire. He seldom went to sleep uneasy or dissatisfied. In fact, he became complacent, lazy, cocooned—cocooned, perhaps, from life itself—by the simple routines he wove around himself.

In later years his satisfaction showed in a broad torso and a full, gray-streaked beard, both of which he sported jauntily. After he became comfortable with the odd act of driving, he became interested in cars, and finally settled—after several trades—on a low-riding vintage convertible, which he also saw restored, though not by his own hand. On Sunday afternoon, after church (he always went to church, although not always to the same church), he cruised the countryside, top down, beard ruffled, a cap over his slightly balding head. And stopped always for supper at his diner, where his waitress—Claire—waited on him, grim and stalwart, always there, always the same.

Claire. Sitting in my leather chair, a shaded lamp throwing light onto the pages of my book—it was the night before her funeral—I thought about Claire. It was hard to imagine her ill, much less dead, yet they'd told me—the bartender, the cook, the other regulars, with whom I'd rarely spoken—that she'd called in sick one night, when I had been out of town for a recital, and then the next had simply not shown up for work. When they called her house, they got no answer; finally, one of her sons had given them the news. I stood there in the diner, not quite sure what to do next, what to say. There was another waitress on duty; I could have sat down at my table, I could have eaten as usual, but of course I didn't. The place suddenly seemed foreign to me, drab, the handwriting on the chalk-board menu childlike, the worn vinyl seats shabby; I saw it through the eyes of a stranger, through the eyes of the friends who had not understood, and now I understood them, and wondered at myself, and left.

She'd died in her sleep, I knew that; she'd been a smoker, and had drunk some, and of course was overweight; probably it had been her heart, the thing that kills so many of us. She was only in her late fifties, not so much older than I, not so different from me at all.

But as I said before, I felt prepared for death. I'd lived next door to it, I'd lived through it; I'd seen the death of my mother, then my father, and then that of young Addison, the embodiment of my expectations, as time rolled by and one by one they fell, fulfilled or not. I was ready, I thought, for death; no ambush could have been better prepared for. Yet, on the night before Claire's funeral, as I sat in the house I owned, among the furniture and books and music I had gathered around me, I could not bear the thought of looking at her face, as I had done my father's; I could not bear the thought that there, too, I might see myself.

And so I stayed away, taught my classes, and went on as if nothing had changed. In a way, nothing has. There's only this: For all those years, I never doubted anything, or knew I was alone. Now, I do.

Happy Father's Day

Late on a Friday night, Frank found himself driving the familiar route, dark trees close on both sides, the sky even darker above, the road swelling into hills beneath him. It was all as he remembered—the old hotels and boarded-up fishing lodges, the mailboxes leaning on posts in uneven rows, the truck that rattled toward him with one headlight out. So much as he remembered it that, as he turned down the long, sloping driveway, he put the car into neutral, and from there let the car coast, quiet, window open to the hissing, briny air. This was how his father had done, each summer when they arrived at the cottage, all the years of Frank's childhood: the car gaining speed at first, then slowing as the land leveled out, and stopping, silent, in front of the garage.

He climbed the stone steps. The door still had no lock. Stepping inside, into the smell of his father—cigarette smoke, bacon, the damp, old age—Frank felt a little like a thief. He walked through, flashlight beam preceding him, and opened each door and looked into each room, until he came to the porch, where the old couch was folded out, made up and waiting, as if his father had been expecting a guest before he was taken to the hospital. Frank dropped his bag, sat on the edge of the bed, and pulled off his shoes. As they fell, he heard water stirring below, somewhere under the floorboards, as the incoming tide washed around the rocks. "Peaceful, peaceful, peaceful," it seemed to say.

His family had used the cottage in Maine as a summer place ever since his grandfather built it more than a century before. Both his grandfather and his father had added on to it over the years, so that, shaded by old trees and steel awnings, it rambled along from one dim, oddly shaped room to the next, and culminated in the porch, a room built on supports over the river, with three walls of windows unshaded from the bright reflections of water and sky. A cove cut into this part of the property, making it U-shaped, a sloping beach at the bottom of the U and the two legs rising into steep ridges. The house stood on one ridge, and the float—a wooden platform resting on four empty oil barrels—lay at the foot of the other. To get from the house to the float, you walked down the stone steps, past the garage, along the beach, up the overgrown, rocky slope and along the opposite ridge, and then down a runway whose pitch could be steep or gentle, depending on the tide.

When he was small, he and his mother and sister spent summers there; his father drove up from Boston on weekends. Over the years, Frank had collapsed all those summers into one, the summer he was eight, when at last he was considered old enough to be on his own. Monday through Friday he did as he pleased, roaming the property, which had three beaches: the one on the river, and two on the ocean, where surf turned boulders to rubble and made caves and pools, where every day new things washed up with the tide and were left behind, glistening and green in the sun—bottles, pieces of pitted metal, dried-up starfish, driftwood. And things that had fallen overboard—a leather shoe, a straw hat, sunglasses, a wooden cigar box, a rubber ball, the husk of an alarm clock. Frank collected seashells, compared them with pictures in his shell book, glued them to one of his father's shirt boards, and made careful labels in his eight-year-old's script.

Early that summer his father had taught him how to handle the flat-bottomed skiff, and so, wearing the life vest his mother insisted on, he rowed out early mornings to sit in the silent fog and fish with a handline, watching for skates to pass underneath him in the shallows, blowing the foghorn occasionally to ward off incoming boats. He learned that a flock of gulls in a frenzy over the water might mean a school of feeding mackerel, boiling just below the surface. He learned how to get a sculpin off his line without sticking himself on its spines. At low tide he took a tin can to the ocean beach and came home with snails to crush open with a rock and use for bait. When he wasn't wandering around, he sat on a lawn chair out on the boardwalk alongside the house and watched the lobster boats go up and down the river. So many times he'd had the urge to row out to one of the buoys—the red one with the white stripe, the solid yellow one that he could see from the porch—and pull it up himself. He could imagine the moment the trap would break water, and how he would feel, waiting to see what was inside.

At fifty, he remembered all of this as clearly as ever, yet could scarcely remember his sister, Joan, being there at all, except for one still life of a young woman lying across a narrow bed, book in hand, mindless of his presence in the doorway. His mother he pictured perpetually in the kitchen, cleaning wild blueberries she'd found somewhere on the property. She tried to make everything perfect the two days his father was there, and partly because of this, and partly because Monday always loomed ahead, the weekends had a frantic feeling, no matter how the time was spent. Late Friday night Frank would wake up to a murmuring in his parents' bedroom, and then Saturday morning to the smell of bacon and pancakes. His mother's plans always revolved around food: huge breakfasts, picnic lunches, clambakes, roast-beef dinners with fancy new desserts. His father responded appreciatively, going on about how poorly he ate at the "greasy spoon" down the street from work, and how he missed her good home cooking. This pleased her, and having done that, his father was free, Frank knew—free to stare at the ocean, to putter around fixing things up, to take Frank on outings.

It was on one Saturday afternoon that Frank's father took him to the wharf in town and introduced him to Charlie (his father pronounced it "Chah-lee," like a Chinese name). Charlie was a young lobsterman, and as the two men talked, Frank stood looking into a galvanized washtub full with that morning's catch, dark lobsters crawling over one another, enmeshed in kelp, and at the wooden traps stacked on the wharf in need of repair and smelling of fish, rotten rope, and salt. "It's all set then, Frank," his father said to him, finally, hand on his shoulder as they left, but it wasn't until dinner that night, when his father told his mother, that Frank knew they were going out with Charlie the next morning. "He'll get sick," his mother said, looking at Frank as if she could already see him growing nauseated, the way he sometimes did in the car on long rides. "No, I won't," Frank said.

The next morning they left the house early, stepping out into partial darkness made gray by fog. Down the steps, across the beach—stones and broken shells crunching underfoot— and up the wet grassy slope, Frank holding on to his father's hand. The tide was so high that the runway to the float was nearly horizontal; a spring tide, his father said, the sun and the moon on the same side of the earth. The gulls were quiet, everything was quiet: even the water, which lapped at the float with kissing noises, seemed quieter than usual. Only his father's voice was close, and real. "If you fall in and drown," he said to Frank, making the joke that forever afterward would be a kind of incantation, "I'll never speak to you again." Then, in the distance, foghorns and the rumble of engines coming nearer.

Now it was his father who was dying, or close to it. Over the phone, the doctor had finally said, "It's age, really. Things begin to fall apart. Your father's nearly ninety." Frank hadn't thought about that, that eighty-nine meant nearly ninety, and that ninety meant close to death. His sister had called and asked him to go: her own health wasn't good; she was older, and it was harder for her to travel, such a long way from Florida to Maine. It had been easy for Frank to pass his clients on to other lawyers in the firm; the office was mostly run by assistants anyway. So he packed up and drove off, leaving Ellen and the kids, who were still in school. He'd come back when he could, he said. He'd come home for weekends, if he could. Ellen said she understood.

When Frank woke at the cottage early Saturday morning, he put on his robe and slippers, fixed himself coffee, and went outside to watch the fog. The deep, cool quiet seemed normal to him, as if the noise he'd become accustomed to in the city was unnatural. Nothing had changed since he was a boy. The beach, its gray stones, the shells of mussels broken into bits where the gulls had dropped them. The faint smell of fish and saltwater. The hollowness of everything, the distant irreality of morning.

Late one morning the summer his last child was born, Frank had stood near this spot and looked down at Ellen, who had fallen asleep in the sun feeding their new daughter—his wife's eyelashes dark on her cheeks, the baby breathing with nose pressed into the downy, milk-filled breast. The other two children were on the beach, playing at the water's edge, in old tennis shoes to protect their feet. Frank had taught the older, Carla, to skip stones, and she was trying to teach four-year-old Manny, who happily lobbed his stones overhand, plunk into the water. But Carla was patient, and showed him over and over again, choosing coinlike bits of stone and sending them gliding out, to touch down and glide again and again.

Frank spent most of that vacation—two weeks near the end of August—with his father, who, when Frank's mother died, had made the cottage his year-round home. He and Frank did everything together, like brothers: made small repairs, chartered a boat and went deep-sea fishing, sat at the kitchen table late into the night, drinking and penciling diagrams onto paper towels, talking about expanding the deck around the house, where to put the new pilings, what to do about the old birch that was in the way. "Build around it," Frank kept saying. "That should be the least of your worries."

One morning they rowed out into the fog to fish for mackerel, which his father said were running at the river's mouth. He'd gotten this tip at the grocery, where he'd gone the night before for cigarettes. ("Why don't you quit smoking?" Frank said. "You want to end up like Mom?" "Why don't you mind your own business?" his father said. "I'll end up as I please.") His father, already in his eighties, had rowed them out, saying, when Frank offered to take the oars, that he didn't like the way Frank jerked the boat around. Only his father could make that old skiff cut through the water silently, dipping the oars edgewise, drawing them back and up with hardly a ripple, his sinewy arms tightening like rubber bands. Once in a while they paused to listen for the surf, the sound that would let them know how close they were to the mouth of the river. The foghorn was Frank's job; he put the clammy mouthpiece to his lips and blew, and other horns answered, making a kind of arhythmic music punctuated by the voices of gulls wheeling overhead. Finally his father pulled the oars in and tied the skiff up to a lobster buoy. For mackerel, they used silvery jigs, dropped over the side from their reels and jerked up and down, back and forth, to resemble something alive. Sure enough, there were mackerel. Time and again, Frank set his hook and rewound the green linen line. The fish looked nearly as metallic as the jigs, but blue-green on top with iridescent patterns on their sides, and bellies almost white. They were like charms for the bracelet of a giant—small, but not too small to eat.

When they'd caught just enough for lunch, they put the reels away. Frank's father ate only fresh fish, and only within hours of its being caught.

The fog had risen to a low ceiling by the time they rowed back, but showed no signs of burning off. Some days it never did, and kept the air cold, damp, and palpable, like a wet rag laid on the skin. Frank rowed so that his father could begin to clean the fish, which he did quickly and with so much agility that Frank worried they'd all be cleaned before they reached shore and the kids wouldn't get to see what one looked like alive. But there were still a few wriggling and whole in the catch pail when they came alongside the float and tied up. Frank carried the pail, his father the clean fish in the ice chest, and the two of them climbed the runway, steep with the low tide.

When they got to the beach, Frank called for the kids to come see the fish. He expected they'd be outside somewhere; it was long past breakfast time. Then he thought they might be inside, playing cards at the old folding table on the porch, or maybe having Ellen read to them, it was such a cool day. He didn't notice that the car was gone until after he'd walked through the house looking for them, then looking for the note that wasn't there. He didn't worry until he noticed the car was gone, and then there was nothing he could do, so he started to wash the dishes, which had been left on the table. As he scrubbed at dried egg yolk, his father reheated what coffee was left in the pot, but it was too bitter to drink, as if it had been boiled. "I'll make you some more," Frank said. His father thanked him.

The two men were sitting on the boardwalk, chairs facing the water, when they heard the car coming down the driveway. They got up and walked down to wait for it. Ellen seemed to be driving with impossible caution, so slowly that Frank doubted his senses. Then finally the car stopped in front of the garage. Feeling as if he were moving through thick water, he went to Ellen's window and looked in. There they were, all four of them: the baby asleep in her car seat, Manny and Carla in the back, huddled in blankets like napping Indians, and Ellen. "It's all right," Ellen said, rolling down her window. "It's all right."

Later she tried to describe his face when he looked into the car, but couldn't. And he couldn't describe what he'd been feeling. It had scared him. As he placed one foot in front of the other, he had been sure, with a kind of deadly cold certainty, that one of them would be gone, that one of them had disappeared while he was fishing with his father, pulling bright things from the water to feed them. And incongruously, he had wondered who would eat the extra fish, if there were any.

What had happened was simple enough: Manny had gone out onto the ledge of rock under the cottage and slipped into the deeper water; Carla had pulled him out. His shoulder ached, his shins and elbows were scraped and forehead bruised, and, as he placidly informed his father, he'd lost a sneaker. But the emergency-room doctor said he was fine. So was Carla, except that she no longer wanted to sleep out on the porch, where all night long she could hear the water moving underneath her, as if breathing in and out.

When his coffee grew cold, Frank got dressed and drove to the hospital thirty miles away. His father was in a room with three other men—all, like him, old and failing. His bed was next to the window, sheets glowing in a flood of sunlight. His eyes were closed. Frank stood next to him, waiting, looking down. He didn't look much different than he had the summer before—a bit thinner maybe. Broken capillaries sketched his nose, his cheeks, as they did the nose and cheeks of every man who spent his time on the water, in the sun and wind. He looked flushed and in an odd way healthy.

Unsure whether to sit in the lone chair and wait, or go and see about getting his father a private room, Frank walked to the foot of the bed and looked at his chart, at the numbers and symbols and abbreviations scribbled there by the doctor, whom Frank knew only as a voice. It didn't mean anything to him, though, and so he was about to leave when his father spoke. "Frank," he said. His eyes were open now. "Yes, Dad, here I am," Frank said. "Been waiting all day for you to wake up."

"Don't lie to me," the old man said. "I heard you come in."

His father didn't want a room alone. He liked to hear the old guys snoring, he said. Besides, they had a bet on who would go first. "It's pneumonia," he said; he spoke slowly, in the same raspy voice but with a new, breathless quality. "No matter what else is wrong. It's pneumonia gets us. I've been reading up on it. Immune system goes; lungs fill up."

There were things to be done to the house, his father said. Frank wrote them down. "You come in the afternoon," his father said. "Around two o'clock. There's no need to stay more than an hour."

"I can come in the morning too," Frank said.

"You work in the morning," his father said. "When you finish that," he moved a finger in the direction of the list, on the back of Frank's checkbook, "I've got more for you."

There was correspondence to be answered; there were bills to be paid, bank accounts consolidated and closed. One afternoon his father asked him to dig through an old filing cabinet. "Nothing's in order," he said. "Look for a big yellow envelope." Among old receipts, insurance policies, photographs, and letters, Frank found the manila envelope: funeral and burial insurance, the receipt for a plot in the local cemetery. "Don't change a thing," his father said.

But he did want his will updated—to include Susan, the baby, now seven years old. Frank's office had drawn it up, so legally Frank could change it; they spent an afternoon going over it. Every day, Frank thought, his father seemed a little stronger, and watching him there in the bed, his face ruddy against the backdrop of white, Frank remembered the day they'd gone out on the lobster boat, in rubber boots and yellow mackinaws—Charlie and his father hauling the traps in, silent except for the commands that Charlie gave now and then, as if the ritual of the catch would be compromised by idle talk. It had been Charlie, his father's friend, who had found him sick in the cottage, when he came by for their card game. It had been Charlie who cleaned the place, made up the couch for Frank to sleep on. It was Charlie who came by mornings to visit, so that Frank could be free to work.

"Charlie still have his lobster boat?" Frank said.

"What's that got to do with your mother's china?" his father said, tapping the papers lying on his lap. "Of course he has."

His father looked close at him; for a moment Frank thought he was starting to cry. Then he remembered that his father's eyes were always full of tears now. "You did love that, didn't you?" his father said.

"What?" Frank said.

"Lobstering."

Frank nodded.

"I know you did," his father said, and turned back to the will.

One morning, Frank had to show a contractor some damage a storm had done to the pilings. The two of them crouched under the house, moving cautiously over the slippery rock, and Frank thought about Manny's accident, on a morning like this seven years before. Low tide had exposed the mysterious underpinnings of the familiar life above, and Frank could see a four-year-old shape moving over the surface of the rock, pausing to touch the barnacle-crusted pilings. He could hear the sister—caught in fear as only a six-year-old can be, between what might happen if she let her brother go and what might happen if she followed—could hear her calling, trying to sound like her mother: "You come back here, Manny!" Then having to go after him. And then, out on the edge where the water was deep, Manny reaching for something—maybe it was only for a sight of the ocean, just around the bend—and sliding into the water, and his sister, openmouthed, plunging her arms in *just* then, at the right moment, and getting hold of his wrist, and pulling, hard, until the head broke water again.

And Frank remembered what he felt when he walked down to the car that morning, waiting to see, unable to hold himself back but unable to move quickly, and his father behind him, saying, "Frank. Don't worry."

Since the house still had no phone, it wasn't until visiting time that afternoon that he knew his father had died. The body had been moved to the funeral home, and as he drove there he felt both constrained and strangely exultant, as if he were facing a difficult decision but already knew what to do, and how to do it. A small man in a dark suit showed him the body. Frank was surprised at how different his father looked, dead. For the first time he looked like someone sick enough to die. "Do you want him to be wearing his glasses?" the mortician said, taking Frank's elbow as they walked from the room. It was a shocking idea.

"No," Frank said. "No. Let him sleep."

Back at the cottage, Frank cleaned the kitchen and bathroom and swept the wide-plank floors and made the beds with fresh sheets, for Ellen and the kids when they arrived. Then he too slept. He dreamed that night of being a lobsterman, his hands moving one over the other again and again, pulling a rope through water and seaweed; the frame of a trap breaking the surface; his hand reaching in; the speckled shell cold, the claws waving; his hand hefting, measuring it, pushing wedges of wood into the flesh—one claw, then the other—and dropping the lobster into a tub with a dozen more scrabbling for position. Alive, all alive. Blanketing them with kelp, to keep the sun off. He saw his hands rebaiting the trap with the foul-smelling chum. He saw his hands drop the trap over the side, watched it sink, the rope playing out of its coil, the green-and-white buoy nodding in the wake of the boat, exactly as he'd seen it that one morning with his father. He saw his hands, rough and large, steering the boat, meeting the waves and coming down on them; he heard the harsh, uneven pounding, like the pounding of a failing heart, and then the all-but-silent breath of the water washing the shore. Then he woke, wondering what his father had dreamed of.

Now, early in June, years after his father's death, Frank sits on the deck with his coffee, listening to a car coming down the driveway, silent save for the crunch of the gravel. Inside, Ellen is making waffles; he can hear her talking to Charlie, who's come over to be there the first time he takes the boat out. "Law to lobsters," Charlie said, grinning when they signed the papers. "Isn't such a leap, I guess." Frank only smiled.

It's early, and cool, and quiet. There's a heavy mist, so he can't see the boat, but he can hear her, bumping the mooring like a mare rubbing her head against the stall door. It's a sound that makes him think ahead. In a moment, the station wagon will glide through the pines and roll to a stop in front of the garage, and his grown children will get out and straggle up the stone steps—Carla in the lead, then Susan, and Manny bringing up the rear, duffel bag pillowing his head. "Happy Father's Day," they'll say; hugs all around, cards and gifts; they'll eat breakfast. And then he'll row them out, the skiff light and smooth on the water, the water clear and cold and deep under them. Eventually the mist will burn off, but it never gets truly warm this early in the season, and he hopes they have the right gear, windbreakers and sweaters and rubber-soled shoes. He hopes they had the sense to pack right.

Horse Dreams

That summer, I began to dream about the horses. My friend had two of them, a Morgan and a quarter horse, and to me they were giant, prehistoric in proportion. I fed them the wet grass that clogged the mower when I mowed the lawn, and their lips on my palm were large and dry. Really, it's no wonder I began to dream about them. When they thudded across the meadow, manes flying, it was definitely mythic. In the stalls they would angle their heads to gaze at me with one eye. Their noses were as long as my arm, their nostrils as big as my mouth. For a week after the Morgan mare was taken away to train, the gelding gave long, melodic neighs, as if sighing or calling her name in the language of horses. He stood alone in the shadow of the barn and looked at me distantly when I held out the grass clippings.

I moved onto my friend's farm near the end of May, and the first dream came on one of those cool June nights that start out clear but end with rain just before dawn. When I woke up, my window was filled with white. A fog had settled in the valley. I fell asleep again, had the dream, and when I woke up the fog had receded to the windbreak, making the trees look distant. I lay there and recalled a watercolor lesson given by a local artist; we had one of his paintings in the living room downstairs. Another summer, fifteen years before this one, my friend and I had been adolescents taking his class together. He taught us tricks: how to use frisket to mask the white and make a real-looking birch tree, how to tilt the wet paper so that the sky was deeper in color at the top, how to make mountains recede into the distance. That was easy: the more vivid the color, the closer the mountains would seem; paler meant farther away.

The moisture and density of the air provided a scientific reason for this, but the effect was psychological as well, since what we see more clearly we assume to be closer. What he taught us was true to life, but somehow not true to art, and I never painted in watercolors again. When the painter died, his little watercolors of an imaginary lake quadrupled in value.

Living on the farm, in the summer of my dreams, I found myself losing interest in music, which had always been important to me in the past. Perhaps this was because music seemed true to art but not true to life. Like a layer of paint on a tree, music was a layer of sound over the sounds of the wind, the animals, the trees. Through the window of my bedroom I could watch the wind as well as hear it, higher currents pushing clouds across the sky or toward us, low winds making the trees rustle even when they seemed motionless. The wind made certain openings in the house and barns behave like whistles emitting a variety of low tones. And since the garden was below my window—bright green rows between mounds of hay and dark unplanted soil—at times I had to lower the shade to avoid being distracted. Of course, often I gave in to it all; on sunny days, I worked on the lawn or in the flower gardens, and I was always the one who watched for the mail and went outdoors to get it, whatever the weather. I would make two piles on the kitchen table, then take mine upstairs to read on my bed. Despite the lure of the outdoors, I became very attached to that room, with the dark paper on the walls and the four posts of the bed, which seemed to lean in over me, and the window framing my view of the land and the weather.

The dreams of the horses did not disturb me. Ironically, it was mostly the gelding I dreamed of—the gelding in my dreams. The dreams were sexual, of course: it didn't take long to decipher their meaning. But none of that was necessary or pertinent. Before coming to the farm, I had dreamed of a neighbor's dog, with its red fur, and, before that, of a scene I had caught on television, of one man making another lick his boot. Sometimes I had another variety of dream, in which I held on to the rope of a tetherball post and swung around and around, touching down as if at the corners of an invisible square. In that dream, it was Easter and the lawn was littered with both dyed eggs and candy eggs wrapped in metallic paper. I picked up one of the candy eggs—it was larger than I'd thought, as large as a goose egg—and unwrapped it to discover that the egg itself was not chocolate but gel, transparent and filled with some clear liquid. When I thought about this dream, what struck me was that both the metallic paper and the shells of the dyed eggs were *colorful,* which settled the old question of whether or not one dreamed only in black and white.

Sometimes I would dream of more ordinary things: leaving telephone messages, speaking aloud, eating a midnight snack. When I woke up, I was never sure if these things had happened or not, but it didn't seem to make any difference. Once I dreamed that I had decided to go to law school, which was an impractical option even at that age, but the dream was so convincing that after I woke up I strode around feeling happily decisive for half the morning, before I realized that the source of my happiness was only a dream. This is a story I like to tell people even today, because it points out that one side of me would like to be more successful, more socially productive. I always end by noting that I could have gone to law school if I had wanted to, but the truth is that I never had any real desire to be a lawyer, or to suffer through three more years of classes and examinations.

Though my friend wanted me on the farm more for company than help, we tried to divide the labor equally, and so the upkeep of the yard fell to me. Soon, images having to do with my mowing the lawn became as important to my dreams as the horses were. I had never had a lawn to take care of before, and had always said that it seemed to me that the mowing of a lawn was another oddment of civilization, like wearing neckties or stockings, or shaving legs and underarms. If one does not want grass two feet high in one's yard, why not install a lower-growing variety of plant? In some parts of the country, lawns are covered with stones or shells, or planted with some sort of vine—something indestructible, like kudzu—and this is considered as attractive as a mown lawn of grass. (I admit, I have seen people in Florida out raking their stones, but some-how that seems less hopeless: stones don't grow, and they more or less stay put; you only have to rake them once a month—perhaps less.) But when I became involved with our lawn, lawns grew to be something of an obsession for me. At first, I would jokingly point out the flaws in other people's yards; then I actually developed an interest in the finer points of trimming and weed prevention. Our lawn was very large and complex, with a good many shrubs. There were plots of perennial flowers in sundry places, a half-dozen old maple trees, a low-hanging crab apple, and a blue spruce that was difficult to get under. Mowing and trimming combined took four hours, more or less, depending on my mood and the weather, and while I was doing it I was aware of almost noth-ing else but the grass I walked over, the variations in the sound of the engine (I could tell when it was about to run out of gas), the blades of the clippers and the stems of plants between them. When I came back to myself, I would suddenly realize that I was hungry, or thirsty, or that my hand was blistered again, or that the sun had burned my back or nose, or that it was nearly dark outside. Finished, I would drag a chair out into the center of the backyard or sit on the swing on the front porch, drink a cold beer, and look at my handiwork. When people visited, I drew their attention to the yard, and saw that trimming in particular was a thankless task, since nobody no-ticed you'd done it, while everyone did if you hadn't. Still, I felt satisfied. It was the only time in my life that I regularly went to bed with dirt under my fingernails.

In my dreams, though, the mowing and trimming were secondary. Lawns themselves became the focus—vast lawns cut short, smooth over rolling hills, almost velvetlike in tex-ture and shine. In the tetherball dream, the eggs rested on nicely cropped grass, and though I never really saw it, I re-member thinking, in that dream, that the grass around the tetherball post was neatly trimmed. In the dreams with the horses, I always saw the grass just on the edge of the paddock. It was eaten short and never needed to be mowed. In my dreams, it looked more like moss than grass, and in reality as well, although I never saw the horses with their noses that low, stuck under the fence to eat the grass. In the horse dreams seeing this grass was almost the only preamble. Usually, my dream made me feel as if I had been reduced to a pair of eyes, floating low over the ground. I recognized the surfaces, and felt myself getting closer to the paddock, then slipping through the boards of the fence. One of the boards had fallen sideways and made a triangle with the other, and I always went through this hole. Then the hoof-pocked mud of the paddock itself, and the breath of the horse. It was the gelding, but he was not a gelding.

These dreams went on for some years, until long after I was married and had children, long after that summer on the farm, that summer of weather and sound. The last time I dreamed of the gelding, we were living in Los Angeles, in a large apartment building. Although the freeway was two blocks away, its hundreds of speeding cars were more than audible over the air-conditioner. I remarked once at dinner that the sound reminded me of mowing the lawn, and one of our guests, pausing between sips of coffee, asked me when I had ever mowed a lawn. In what life? And I myself found it hard to believe— hard to know what was memory, and what dream.

Someone

Around the first of June, I moved into the new house. I had no curtains for the big picture windows in the living room, so I draped a bedspread across the front one. The one on the side I left uncovered and put the TV in front of. This meant that when I sat on the couch watching television, I could also look out across the yard at my neighbors, the Mabees.

Mr. Mabee had once been in construction supply. I knew this because I'd found an old invoice on a shelf in my garage: it listed a pound of nails and some wood. Mrs. Mabee I had no idea about. She was skeletal, loose skinned, not much hair and long hands that gestured or held her elbows. She seemed to spend most of her time hanging laundry out to dry or taking it down; she had a short line on the front porch and a several-tiered longer one in the backyard. Mr. Mabee, retired from the construction-supply business, worked as a traffic cop, putting tickets on illegally parked cars and cars whose meters had run out. But he seemed to spend most of his time on his mower, which he also used as a small tractor. He took care of a huge garden in the backyard and mowed the lawn twice a week all summer. Since their lawn abutted my driveway, and since my windows were always open, I heard him every morning. When he gave out tickets, he wore dark blue: a short-sleeve shirt, baggy pants, a cop's hat. But on the tractor he wore a white T-shirt and sparkling clean painter's overalls. Mrs. Mabee wore spongy knits—pants with elastic waists and nylon tops, what we used to call shells. Their own clothes never seemed to turn up on the lines; I used to watch someone's jeans and boxer shorts and the sheets hang in the breezeless heat.

I'd had my hair cut short that summer, for the first time since I was a child. When the heat really set in, I'd wake up in the morning with it in spikes. Often I didn't bother with it, went around like that all day. My landlady, Helen, would come over to take care of the flowers or to bring me something, sachets of potpourri or a new broom, and I'd find her looking at my hair instead of in my eyes, and then I'd realize that I hadn't done anything about it. Still, I didn't much care. Some days I only got dressed because it was a small town and people tended to drop by unannounced. Even when I got the curtains up in the living room, I felt people watching me when I was in the kitchen or on the sun porch. So I put on a pair of nylon shorts and a T-shirt. Later in the summer I cut the sleeves and collars off most of the T-shirts, the way teenagers were doing, and this was a lot more comfortable.

On alternate days, I ran. At dawn I woke up to the sound of the construction crew digging up the blacktop they had laid down the day before, and put on my new gray running shoes. These shoes were full of air, they were so light they felt invisible, they made my feet feel alive and free. I'd run right out the front door, down the little broken sidewalk, past the Mabees' house, downtown—past the gas stations, the little closed shops, the park. Up to the college, around the campus, past the white Victorian houses with their shining glass windows. The kind of town this was, there were dozens of people running around at this time of day, just before the heat made breathing difficult, and we all smiled and waved to one another. But generally I had to pay pretty close attention to what I was running on, so that I wouldn't catch my foot, twist my ankle, and fall. I hated to fall. I hated humiliation of any kind.

Often I would run too far and end up walking home in the heat, but this was all right because it took longer and made it so I didn't have to waste more of the morning. I'd take my bath, put on clean shorts and T-shirt, and make lunch of yogurt and wheat germ and juice and a number of vitamin pills, each designed to attack what I viewed as a serious health problem. For instance, my hair was falling out, which was the reason I had cut it: I thought maybe the weight had become too much, after all those years. Also, my skin was too dry, and my nails came in corrugated. I got my information from Earl Mindell's *Vitamin Bible,* which I bought at the college bookstore.

After lunch I would take something to read and sit on the olive green metal chair that had come with the house, out in the backyard in the midday sun. Sometimes I'd wear a big brimmed hat I'd bought in the Bahamas, a straw thing with stripes, but generally I just let the sun beat down on my face. It beat at an angle, since I was sitting up and reading, so that my nose and cheeks were burnished while the area under my chin remained pale. It hurt my eyes to read in the sun like that, the black words boiling on the white page, but I was oblivious to everything but the story at hand, and sat out there until my body began to demand rehydration. Then I went inside to drink some sweet, cold iced tea. I always kept a gallon of it made up in an old industrial-size mayonnaise jar.

By four or so I was exhausted. Sometimes I would take a beer and pull all the blinds and close the curtains and watch TV in the dim living room. I got only one channel, the public station, so I watched "Sesame Street" or yoga with the sound off, and drank my beer. I needed to relax by four in the afternoon. What I wanted to do was cook dinner, but if I cooked dinner and ate it too early, the evening would seem to wear on forever. So I sat on the old couch drinking the beer and watching the soundless images. Sometimes I got on the floor and pretended to follow the movements of the yoga lady, who beamed with health and serenity. I admired her hair, a long, thick, black braid, something like mine before I got it cut, before it began to fall out.

Sometimes I would fall asleep when I did the relaxation bit with her at the end of the show. This was the best thing that could happen, because then sometimes I slept through dinner-time and into the dark, and when I woke up hours later, I would just eat more yogurt and go to bed with a book.

But when I didn't fall asleep, I watched TV mindlessly until the news came on. I could not enjoy watching the news, with this man's head centered in the screen looking at me, his mouth moving without meaning because I would not turn the sound on, because if I turned up the sound I would hear the news.

That I didn't want. So when the news came on, I would change
to a channel of snow and get out my tape deck. I had one of
those portable units, and sometimes I would pretend to be a
black teenager and put the thing on my shoulder and dance
around the living room with my ear being blasted out. On one
wall of the living room was a big mirror where I could watch
the movements of my ever-slimmer hips. More than once, I
rolled my eyes at myself. I could lose myself in this dancing
for an hour or more, and then, usually, it was late enough that
I could start dinner, an elaborate, slow process during which I
did not allow myself one bite until the meal was on the table.
I did drink some wine while I cooked; it made the preparations
last longer, leaving less time later in the evening.

The things I ate! Money was no problem, so Thursdays I
would stop at the fish truck, parked by the park, and buy
some shrimp or even a lobster. I had three new cookbooks—
Chinese, Italian, and French—and I tried an unfamiliar recipe
every few days or so, cutting the measurements down to make
everything for one: one serving, one person, no leftovers. I
made miniature loaves of whole wheat bread, quarter-dozens
of buttery dinner rolls. I made tiny pies: raspberry, blueberry,
strawberry-rhubarb. When I went to the market, I looked for
seasonal specials. I never bought anything frozen or canned or
in boxes: I didn't want to save time. This meant I went to the
market frequently. Often I stopped on my way home from
running.

I set the table with crystal, china, the real silver. A taper in
the silver candlestick. Wildflowers picked from the wild field
behind my house. A lace tablecloth. Everything was as elegant
as if I were in a fine restaurant or at an expensive wedding
reception. I made myself pâté, I bought little cans of caviar. I
grew basil plants, dill, chives. On Sundays, I watched the
gourmet cooking shows on public television and wrote the
recipes down. I never made the same thing twice or bought
enough of anything that it would go bad or I'd get tired of it.
Except wine—I bought that by the case.

By the time I had prepared the meal, dressed for dinner
(every night in the same white sundress), eaten, cleared, and
cleaned up, it was dark, even when the sun set as late as nine-

thirty or ten. Then I took my coffee out onto the sun porch and sat there, or on the back stoop, and listened to the insects and smelled the summer air. There was a bar across the street from the house, and even though I couldn't see it from the sun porch, which was around back, I could hear the music and laughing, people getting into and out of their cars, and I could picture the neon beer signs red and blue against the dark. I'd sit there a long time, and think. My stomach was content, my body tired, but I couldn't shut my mind up, and I would just think, and think, going around in green circles of thought, wondering where people were and what they were doing, the people I had known. Of course, there were particular people I thought about more than others. I felt like an exile or a patient sent away for the cure. Even though I was living exactly as I wanted, even though it was the peak of beautiful summer, I couldn't stop thinking. Perhaps I shouldn't have drunk the coffee.

Then, one night as I sat in shadow on the back steps, I saw Mrs. Mabee come out of her house. It was a cloudy, muggy night, no moon or anything, but there was enough light from the streetlamps to see her, vaguely, and to know that she was carrying a basketful of laundry in her arms. It was close to midnight. I watched her take the sheets, the T-shirts, the men's shorts and jeans from the basket—they were heavy, dripping—and shake and then lift them up to the line and pin them there with clothespins she took from the pouch of her apron. She moved down the long line and then began the second tier, and it took half an hour for her to finish. Then she picked up the empty basket with one hand and went back inside, just as if it were morning and time to fix her husband breakfast.

I was having a dream that night when the storm hit, and it took me a while to remember where I was, to understand what was happening. There was a wind, and my living room was alive, crackling with light and violence. A branch had fallen on the electric wires in front of the Mabees' house. My television screen flashed and went dark; the stink of sulphur came through the open windows, the flapping curtains. Then the noise and light stopped and the streetlamps went out, making it seem as if there were no town around me at all, only the steady drumming presence of rain, rain. By the flame of a candle I called the power company and got a man who sounded as if he was completely awake, expecting my call. Yes, he said. Someone was on his way.